spring into murder

Alaska Cozy Mystery
Book Five

wendy meadows

Majestic Owl Publishing LLC
P.O. Box 997
Newport, NH 03773

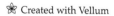 Created with Vellum

chapter one

The snow was gone – for now, at least. The yard surrounding Sarah's cabin was sprouting with life and beauty. Of course, to Sarah, the ground still felt frozen and her bones were cold from a long, hard, winter. But it was nice to be able to step outside without her ears freezing off and her face turning into a mask of ice. "I still love the snow, though," Sarah smiled, stepping outside and closing the front door to her cabin. She drew in a deep breath of warm, fresh air, listened to the sweet sounds of the musical birds, studied the lush, green blossoming trees surrounding her land, and then smiled again. "The snow can wait for a bit. But my day of shopping can't."

Sarah lazily watched the wind play with the long-sleeved blue and white dress she was wearing. The wind ruffled across her dress for a few moments and then ran its fingers through her soft, recently shampooed hair. She loved the way the wind felt, she loved the wilderness that surrounded her home, and she loved the way Alaska felt like home. Sure, since she had moved to Snow Falls there had been some serious problems, beginning with the menacing snowman she found in her yard wearing a black leather jacket and chewing on a peppermint candy cane. And sure, Conrad had faced off with a deadly mafia killer. And then there was the problem with the dead forest ranger and Conrad's old friend in Minnesota. But all of those things were in the past. Spring had arrived and Sarah was determined to put the long, dark winter she had fought against behind her. "Time to go shopping," she said and began walking toward her Subaru. She hadn't gotten far when her friend Amanda pulled into the driveway.

"Hey, you!" Amanda waved at Sarah as she jumped out of her truck wearing the brightest yellow dress Sarah had ever seen in her life. "Where are you off to?"

Sarah sighed. She loved her best friend; she adored her best friend; she would even die for her best friend. But why did she have to dress like a neon sunflower? "Where did you find that dress?" she asked, walking up to Amanda's truck.

Amanda glanced down at the yellow dress. "You don't like?" she asked in a curious, offended voice, assuming a fake German accent.

"Well," Sarah winced, "it's...the color...the material is...kinda bright."

"I know," Amanda beamed. "My dear hubby hates this dress. So I picked this wonderful, delightful...very annoying...gift out of my closet simply to annoy him, the poor dear." Amanda smiled triumphantly.

Sarah fought back a smile. "How is his leg?" she asked.

"Still in a cast," Amanda replied. She folded her arms together. "I told that hard-headed dumbbell to stay off the roof, did I not?"

"You did."

"Did that hard-headed dumbbell listen to his wife?"

"He didn't," Sarah replied, watching her best friend's face turn bright red anew with anger.

"And what happened to him, you might ask?"

"Your husband slipped and fell off the roof and broke his leg," Sarah finished for Amanda.

Amanda nodded her head up and down, up and down, until it seemed like it might go flying off into space. "And who gets to become his personal maid?"

"You."

"That's right, love, me. Dear old, poor old, Amanda." Amanda rolled her eyes. "Get me this, get me that, I need help going to the bathroom...oh, my leg hurts...I'm hungry...fetch me the newspaper...get the tv remote for me...where's my crossword...Oh!" Amanda slammed her truck door closed behind her with frustration.

"I take it you're here because you needed some fresh air?"

"I'm here because I want to go shopping with you, love," Amanda forced a smile to her face. "O'Mally's Department Store is selling off its winter stock at 70% off." Amanda grinned. "Ready to fight the crowds?"

"I doubt there will be any crowds to fight off, Amanda. This is Main Street in Snow Falls, Alaska we're talking about, it's hardly Fifth Avenue," Sarah pointed out.

Amanda made a pouty face. "Can't we at least pretend there will be a huge mob to fight through?" she begged Sarah.

Sarah smiled. "Sure. I'll even go back inside and get my gun. I'll fight off the horde while you shop."

"That's my girl," Amanda beamed. "After dealing with my husband for two solid weeks, I need this so badly."

Sarah laughed. "Let's say I just leave my gun at home, take you shopping, and then treat you to lunch?"

"Deal," Amanda smiled. She grabbed Sarah's hand and pulled her toward the truck. "I'll drive. My truck has more room for goodies."

Sarah didn't argue. She climbed into the passenger's seat, buckled up, and waited for Amanda. A relaxed feeling entered her heart. "This is going to be a nice morning," she whispered as her eyes rested on her cabin. The cabin seemed at peace, surrounded by the untamed wilderness, at one with the land.

An hour later Sarah found herself inside O'Mally's Department Store going through a rack of women's winter sweaters. To Amanda's disappointment, the store was only half full of easy-going shoppers, none of whom had the least desire to brawl over a few sensible sweaters. But in contrast to Amanda, Sarah found the store's quietude merely relaxing and fun. "What about this one?" she asked and held up a dark green sweater with a soft yellow line zig-zagging across the middle.

Amanda studied the sweater with careful, curious eyes. "Ah...no," she finally said and shook her head.

Sarah examined the sweater. "I guess you're right," she agreed and put the sweater back on the clothing rack. Amanda picked up a soft pink sweater. "I like it," Sarah said. "Pink is your color."

Amanda smiled and draped the sweater over her arm with a few other lucky finds. "So," she said looking up and down the clothing aisle, "when is Conrad getting back from New York?"

Sarah glanced at Amanda. She figured the subject of Conrad would come up sooner or later. "Next week."

"Oh, that soon, huh?" Amanda asked. She picked up another soft pink sweater and added it to the pile on her arm. "Has he...called?"

Sarah sighed, knowing her friend wanted all the gossip but was too polite to come out and say so. "Conrad called me last night."

"Oh, that's nice," Amanda replied with uncharacteristic restraint.

Sarah smiled and fingered a dark brown sweater. Amanda crinkled her nose and shook her head no. "Conrad asked me to tell you hello," she told Amanda and passed the brown sweater by.

"That's nice," Amanda said and grinned at Sarah. "Anything else?"

"No," Sarah told Amanda and cheekily tossed a white sweater at her. Amanda caught it, examined the style, and nodded. "Is that one my color?"

"Yes," Amanda said and lovingly piled it together with the others she had gathered. "Are you sure Conrad didn't say anything else...like maybe...I miss you?"

"Maybe we should walk over to the sporting goods department and get you a fishing pole and a hook," Sarah teased Amanda.

"Oh, come on, love," Amanda pouted, "I just want to know if you two...you know...are becoming closer."

"In time," Sarah promised. "I like Conrad, I really do. He's a good guy. And maybe...in time...we'll become more than friends. But for now," Sarah cautioned Amanda, "my heart isn't ready to dive into romance. I'm comfortable in my life. I'm...getting used to the idea of being a divorced woman."

"Fair enough," Amanda said and backed off.

Sarah gave Amanda a grateful look. "Thanks—" she began to say but stopped when she saw Andrew walking up. Andrew was wearing a serious expression on his face. "Oh no," she whispered.

"Ladies," Andrew said, straightening the jacket of his crisp Chief of Police uniform. Although it made him look professional, Sarah could see that deep down, Andrew felt silly and out of place without his usual police department parka and blue jeans; and boy, did the starch in that uniform look like it made his skin itch.

"We're off duty," Amanda admonished him and grabbed Sarah's arm. "Let's go."

Sarah bit down on her lower lip and was too startled to protest as Amanda rushed them away. But Andrew tugged at his collar and then gave chase. "Now, wait a minute," he begged, jogging to keep up with them through the displays of clothing in the women's department.

"Not even a second," Amanda called out over her

shoulder. She dragged Sarah and her armful of sweaters around a hard corner and hurried toward Intimates, taking a gamble. Surely Andrew wouldn't follow them into the bra department.

Andrew slid to a stop as he realized where Amanda had led the chase, scratched at his starchy collar again, and sighed. "I can wait," he promised.

Sarah looked over her shoulder. She spotted Andrew trying to scratch his pants leg surreptitiously. Pity entered her heart. Andrew was a good man. A good husband. A good cop. "Maybe we better see what Andrew wants?" she asked Amanda, who had begun looking through a rack of slips with feigned interest.

"Oh," Amanda said as she stomped the tan carpet under her feet, forgetting the slips for the moment. "Why? We were having such a pleasant morning."

"I know," Sarah agreed, "but look at him standing over there, scratching himself...looking like a lost puppy."

Amanda studied Andrew. "The poor bloke does appear pitiful." Her heart caved in. "Oh...alright. But you still owe me half a girls' day out!"

"Deal." Sarah took Amanda's hand and walked back to Andrew. "We're all ears."

Andrew stopped scratching at his pants leg hurriedly when he saw them approach and seemed relieved. But Sarah could also see that bad news was waiting for her. "A group of bird watchers were out hiking earlier this morning and came across a dead body. A hunter, it seems."

"I knew it," Amanda fussed.

"Now, wait just a minute," Andrew cautioned, "the body showed no signs of foul play. It appears this man got himself lost and froze to death. It also appears he's been frozen for a long time, too."

"So, what do you need with me?" Sarah asked Andrew.

"Well," Andrew said, "the body belongs to a man named William Archie Hopski..."

"Which means you found identification on the body," Sarah said.

Andrew nodded. "If the man had been murdered, I'm pretty sure I wouldn't have found his wallet with an ID, never mind that it was full of money."

"If you don't think this Mr. Hopski was killed, why bother us?" Amanda asked again. Sarah suppressed a smile. She could tell that despite her fussing, her best friend was secretly intrigued already.

Andrew tugged at his shirt collar again. "Darn starch," he muttered.

"Mrs. Tarrington does go heavy on the starch," Sarah agreed.

"I should arrest her," Andrew said with a roll of his eyes. "Listen, Sarah, Mr. Hopski wasn't a young buck. The man was ninety-two years old. He is, or rather was, extremely – and I mean extremely – wealthy." Andrew pulled a small notepad out of his pocket and consulted his notes. "There's a missing person report out on him in Los Angeles. He's been missing since December of last year. Now either the man got lost and froze to death or had himself a heart attack. But my guess is he got himself lost."

"Why is that?" Sarah asked.

"Just a hunch, I guess," Andrew confessed. "He was found near a trail system that heads down a series of foothills toward town, so my guess is that he was headed back. More importantly, I also found an empty bag of beef jerky in his right coat pocket and an empty canteen next to his body. Unlikely he was headed out with no supplies, unless he was senile. And the missing person report makes no mention of anything like that."

Sarah considered the evidence. "Any weapons on him?"

"I found his rifle lying a few feet from the body," Andrew

nodded. "It's likely that the rifle might have been disturbed by wind or snow or even a curious bear. But it was there. He had his hunting license in his wallet."

"Maybe the fright of being lost gave the poor old man a heart attack?" Amanda suggested, lost in thought and resting her pile of sweaters on top of a nearby clothing rack. "I know if I became lost I sure wouldn't be singing happy campfire songs."

"Could be," Andrew agreed, looking at Amanda. "I'll know the cause of death once I get the coroner's report." Andrew focused on Sarah. "Sarah, Mr. Hopski's three children are flying up to our little town here, angrier than wet hornets. One of them already tried to strongarm me into releasing the body, but I told them the state has very strict guidelines about performing an autopsy first, and I don't have the authority to override that, no matter what. Also, Mr. Hopski's wife...a younger woman...is joining the bandwagon. These people are city folk from Los Angeles, your neck of the woods. So, you see..."

"Oh, I understand," Sarah said, humoring Andrew with a smile. "You want me to deal with the cappuccino drinking, freeway hogging, snotty brats and their diva of a stepmother who are all storming up to our cozy little corner of Alaska from the bright lights of Los Angeles?"

"Please," Andrew begged. "I can starch my good uniform stiff as a board and I'll still be just a small-town hick to these people." He looked at Amanda. "You're a big city woman from London. You can help Sarah, too."

Amanda raised an eyebrow. "Well, I wouldn't call myself a big city woman anymore, but I do know how to handle the wild streets of London," Amanda stated in a proud voice. She looked at Sarah. "It seems like our services are needed, love. We can't leave poor Andrew in a bind, now can we?"

"And neglect performing our civic service for our fair

community? No way," Sarah told Amanda. She winked at Andrew. "Okay, Chief, we'll help you out. What's your plan?"

"I have to wait until I get the official cause of death," Andrew explained in a grateful voice. "In the meantime, I'm swearing you two ladies in as my official Public Relations team."

"Public Relations, I like it," Amanda said happily. "Oh, it's a shame that this is going to give me an excuse...I mean require me to take more time away from my dear hubby. Just think, my ears will be free of that blasted bell. Oh, the joy of it all."

Sarah felt a smile touch her lips. Sure, a man had been found dead, but for once she wasn't needed for a murder investigation. No, what Snow Falls needed was a cultural ambassador who could negotiate between the little town and the city folk. However, her gut told her that the incoming visitors weren't motivated by grief or anguish; a rich man with a young wife and three children from a big city spelled more to do with greed, in her experience. She only hoped that she was wrong. "Call us when the war party arrives."

"Hey, thanks ladies," Andrew said in a relieved voice and scratched at his trouser leg again. "I better get back down to the station. I'll be in touch." Leaning down to scratch more urgently at his knee, Andrew backed up into a display of silky nightgowns, eliciting a gasp from the passing Mrs. Turner and giggles from the few other nearby shoppers. "Oh, sorry," he said, his face turning bright red as he tried to pick up the fallen nightgowns hurriedly.

"Andrew, what would your mother say?" said Mrs. Turner, indignantly swinging her hard-sided black purse into his arm as she swept past him.

"Uh...Mrs. Turner, I didn't see you. Have a nice day," Andrew said lamely, rubbing his arm. "For seventy-eight years old, that woman sure packs a wallop," he muttered as he stalked off toward the exit.

Amanda grinned as she turned to catch Sarah's reaction to this. Sarah barely held back a laugh. "Well, Amanda, looks like our day out may not be interrupted after all. We still have plenty of time to get lunch at the diner before our PR services are needed."

Amanda smiled happily as they set off through the sale racks once again. "You know," Amanda said in a curious voice as she lingered at a display of wool socks, "I wonder what kind of mess we're getting ourselves into now?"

"As long as it's not murder," Sarah pointed out and walked Amanda back to the sweater rack.

"Ah, but a man was found dead," Amanda replied and focused on a bright green sweater that she knew her husband would despise and quickly tossed it onto the growing pile on her arm.

"True," Sarah admitted and bit down on her lower lip to avoid commenting on the outrageous green sweater. "But," she continued, "Mr. Hopski was found dead with his canteen empty, no food, a wallet full of money, and his rifle. I'd surmise that the poor man got lost and froze to death. It's even possible the fear of being lost gave him a heart attack, like you suggested. But..."

"But what?" Amanda asked in a quick voice. "Come on, love, don't hold back on me."

Sarah picked up a pretty teal sweater and held it against her body, considering. "Andrew didn't say he found any medication on the deceased."

Amanda shivered. "Call him Mr. Hopski, love...when you say 'deceased' I feel all creepy inside."

"Andrew would have told us if he found any heart medication," Sarah said and Amanda approvingly placed the teal sweater on the pile in her arms. "We need that coroner's report to know more. And...I hate to say this, but I think we need to cut our shopping trip short. I need to go make a few calls."

"I kinda figured you were going to say that," Amanda pouted. "But at least use the payphone at the diner, okay love, because this woman's stomach is beginning to complain."

"I admit, a greasy cheeseburger does sound good right about now," Sarah grinned and winked at Amanda. "Lunch is on me."

"Then what are we waiting for?" Amanda said brightly and hustled toward the registers with her armful of sweaters. Sarah followed, wondering who Mr. Hopski really was, and what had brought him to this small town in rural Alaska from big city Los Angeles. Her detective's mind was curious and turning over every clue as she watched her best friend's purchases being wrapped in tissue paper then placed in a shopping bag. They needed lunch, but they also needed information.

Peter Greenfield walked into his office just in time to hear the phone ringing. He tossed a take-out container of Chinese noodles down onto his desk and snatched up the phone. "Greenfield," he said in a gruff voice.

"It's lunch time, so let me guess: noodles from Mr. Chen's Chinese Palace?" Sarah spoke softly.

"You're good, kid," Pete said and plopped down into his desk chair with a chuckle as he pushed aside a pile of folders and papers. He opened the box of noodles and dug in with his plastic fork. "So, to what do I owe the honor? Or should I just ask what you want?"

A twinge of guilt struck Sarah. She paused as she looked down the short hallway in the rear of the diner and saw Amanda studying the menu at their booth. The smell of coffee, cheeseburgers, and meatloaf was calling out to her stomach, even though she was standing at a pay phone located unfortunately close to the bathrooms. "Maybe I should send you a box of cigars first?"

"Maybe you should get your butt back to Los Angeles and get back to work, Detective," Peter quipped. Despite the humor in his voice, she could also plainly hear the fatigue. Through the phone she heard him as he dropped the plastic fork back into the noodles and rubbed a tired hand over his face.

"Oh, Pete," Sarah replied miserably, "I hate to break it to you, but you know that part of my life is over."

"Sure it is," Peter huffed. "Seems to me you're solving more murders up there with the polar bears than you ever did down here in the bright sunshine."

"I..." Sarah paused. How could she refute Peter's statement? It was obvious her old friend was in a bad mood and she knew better than to press him. "Maybe I should call back later..."

"Sure, that'll happen." By the tone in his voice, she could envision him rolling his eyes. "And by the way, why didn't you call my cell?"

"I lost my cell phone in the snow," Sarah confessed. "I was moving snow in my driveway and—"

"Sure, sure, never mind," Peter replied impatiently. "What do you want, kid? Some of us are still cops, you know," Peter snapped and then immediately softened. "Hey, Sarah, I didn't mean that...it's just been a tough day, you know how it is. Two bystanders took a bullet during a bank robbery that one of my guys tried to prevent."

"I'm sorry."

"So am I," Peter replied. He shook his head. "Sometimes I think I'm ready to throw this job into the trash and move up there with the polar bears myself."

"You'll never leave Los Angeles, Pete. We both know that. You wouldn't be able to drive that vintage convertible Chevrolet of yours much in the snow. Not much surfing up here, either. Who's going to admire your tan when you're bundled up in a parka?"

Peter gave a brief chuckle. Sarah was relieved that at least her friend was still able to laugh. "Yeah, yeah," he said and shifted gears. "You want a favor. What is it?"

Sarah missed her old friend more than she could ever admit. "A man by the name of William Archie Hopski was found dead early this morning. It appears the cause of death was exposure to cold, no foul play that we know of yet. But Pete, I need to know who this man is. He had a missing person report filed in Los Angeles County. If you can run a check for me, I sure would owe you."

"You owe me too much already," Peter reminded Sarah. He grabbed a stained mug full of lukewarm coffee and took a drink. "But I don't need to run a check on Mr. Hopski, kid. I can tell you all about the man myself."

"Really? How come I've never heard of him before?"

"Neither had I until the man came up missing," Peter explained. "Mr. Hopski is a wealthy realtor, Sarah. He sold mansions to the so-called stars and bought up a lot of land in the fancy hills that he gradually sold off. The man has a net worth of over four billion dollars."

Sarah whistled low, taken aback.

"Ever hear of Sun Wave Realty?" Peter asked.

Sarah thought back to her life in Los Angeles and roamed around the city in her memory. "As a matter of fact, I remember seeing billboards with that name."

"Los Angeles has a thousand and one realtors," Peter told Sarah. "Mr. Hopski only sold to the so-called upper crust who could dish out twenty million for a mansion without batting an eye. We're not talking about a man who sold middle-class homes to hard working families."

Sarah made a few mental notes. "Pete, Mr. Hopski's three children and his wife are on their way up to my little town as we speak. Can you throw any information on them my way?"

Pete finished off his coffee and winced at the bitter flavor. "Got some paper on you?"

"I have my memory."

"Good girl," Peter said and began going down a list of names in his mind. "Okay, the old man had three kids. Two boys, and a girl. The oldest is Natalie Hopski. She's sixty years old. Watch out for her."

"Why's that?"

"The woman has never been married so she's not a black widow, exactly...but rumors have always followed her," Peter warned.

"Thanks, Pete. I get it."

"Good. Now, the second oldest is Chet Hopski. The guy is fifty-five years old, and like his sister, lives off his old man's dime. Chet is married to a woman named Teresa, no children, and is about as smart as a skunk crossing the road."

"He's the opposite of his sister, I take it?"

"You bet," Peter confirmed. "Last we have Milton Hopski, age fifty. Milton has been divorced five times, lives off his old man's dime like his brother and sister, and back in December was dating a woman who could turn out to be his sixth wife, if you can believe that. Milton has some brains to him, like his older sister, so watch out for him."

"What about Mr. Hopski's wife?"

"Ah," Peter said and rolled his eyes in disgust. "Charlene Nelton."

"By the tone of your voice, I take it the girl is pretty young?"

"Charlene is thirty-one years old," Peter said. "They married when she was in her twenties. Charlene Nelton isn't a model or an actress or a singer or any of those things."

Sarah cleared her throat. "Okay...so what is she? Besides pretty?"

"She's rich," Peter replied. "Charlene Nelton is the daughter of Ned Nelton, the owner of the Green Foods grocery store chain. Ned Nelton is worth quite a bit of dough, kid."

"How did Charlene meet Mr. Hopski? ...Wait, I think I can guess. Mr. Hopski sold Ned Nelton a mansion, right?"

"Nice to hear you're still sharp as a tack," Peter replied. "Four years ago, Hopski and his young bride tied the knot shortly after her old man bought a mansion from Hopski."

"A real gold digger, huh, Pete?"

Peter studied his stuffy office. "Charlene Nelton is after power *and* money, kid. She's the kind of dangerous woman who wants to get her dirty hands into politics. Marrying Hopski was her way of gaining more power. All I know is that the mayor's office got involved in the missing persons report at some point, and that doesn't happen every day. Somebody pulled some strings."

"I see," Sarah said and bit down on her lower lip. "And I take it Natalie and Charlene don't exactly see eye to eye?"

"Ever put a scorpion and a black widow spider in the same tank?"

"That bad, huh?" Sarah asked.

"You bet," Peter confirmed. "But hey," he added in a grateful voice, "they're your problem now, Detective Garland." Peter chuckled to himself. "Who would have thought that this department's biggest headache would end up in your lap? Serves you right, too, for leaving us in the lurch."

"I guess it does," Sarah agreed.

"No, it doesn't," Peter softened his voice. "I'm just teasing."

"I miss you like crazy, Pete," Sarah admitted. She wiped a tear out of her eye. "I wish you would come spend some time with me."

"Too busy, kid," Peter told Sarah in a regretful voice. "I have a bank robber to track down."

"I understand."

"I know you do," Peter assured Sarah. "But hey, listen, I have my two weeks coming up at the end of summer. Maybe I'll come up and see you then."

"Really?" Sarah asked in an excited voice.

"You know me," Peter smiled, "always vacation in autumn when—"

"The world is cooling down, I know," Sarah smiled, remembering his perennial words.

Peter smiled again. "Okay, kid, I better get off the horn and get back to work. Call me if you encounter any problems."

"I'll call you even if I don't," Sarah promised. "I...I miss you, Pete. If you mean what you just said about paying me a visit then you just made me the happiest girl in the world."

"I meant it," Peter told Sarah. "Now, enough with the mushy stuff. Take a hike and get to work." Peter ended the call. He stared at the phone where it sat on his desk and sighed. "I miss you, too, kid," he whispered and tried to focus on his work and his lunch again.

Sarah walked out of the hallway and sat down across from Amanda. "Well?" Amanda asked, still studying the menu.

"It's not the Partridge Family coming to town, that's for sure," Sarah explained and casually looked around the diner. The diner decor was a mix of rustic log cabin and 1950s café. The walls were made of rough-sawn logs but the floor was black and white checkered tile. Photos of old country singers lined the walls while a shiny antique jukebox sat pushed up against the back wall. The jukebox was playing 'Crazy,' an old song by Patsy Cline. Aside from Sarah and Amanda, a few other hungry patrons were sitting in the booths, talking and eating without being too noisy or noticeable. It was a cozy place that they returned to time and again, the kind of place that the locals knew and loved very well.

"I think it's time I renovated my coffee shop and made it appealing like this diner," said Sarah, looking around approvingly.

Amanda didn't argue. As much as she loved her best friend, Sarah knew that Amanda privately thought the coffee shop was an eyesore. "Good ideas are born every day," Amanda told Sarah with a wink. "So...if we're not getting the Partridge Family, who are we getting?"

"Bad news," Sarah said and shook her head. "Amanda my dear, you and I are going to have our hands full. My old friend in Los Angeles implied we should be ready for four gold-digging loose nuts." Sarah picked up the menu and began reading through the food options, even though she already knew her favorites. "I think I'll have a cup of coffee, a cheeseburger, and some french fries."

"I'm going with the meatloaf," Amanda told Sarah and drew in a deep, contented breath. "Is it wrong to love a meatloaf?" she teased.

A short, plump woman wearing a blue and white uniform dress walked up to the booth. "Hello, Anne," Sarah smiled at the server. "How is Mr. Rainy today?"

"Grouchy as ever," Anne Rainy replied and tossed a thumb over her shoulder toward the kitchen. "Who can talk to him when he's in one of his moods?" Anne looked at Amanda. "How's your husband's leg coming along?"

Amanda made a put-upon face. "The sound of that awful bell he uses to summon me will haunt my dreams for years to come."

Anne nodded with a chuckle. "When Wilson broke his leg, oh...ten years ago I'd say? He nearly drove me to the mad house ringing his bell all the time. I nearly made him go sleep out in the snow."

Sarah smiled. Anne Rainy was a hardscrabble woman

with a gentle heart. Even though her face never smiled, her eyes always expressed what she was feeling. "Is it safe to order a cup of coffee and a cheeseburger plate?"

Anne looked over her shoulder and studied the door leading into the kitchen. "As long as you don't mind your burger burnt to a crisp around the edges." Sarah winced but nodded.

"How about the meatloaf?" Amanda dared to ask. "I've been smelling it since we walked in and my stomach won't stop growling!"

Anne looked down at Amanda. "Meatloaf is fine," she said and smiled with her eyes. "You want coffee, too?"

"Sure," Amanda smiled and put her menu away. "And I'll have a slice of your famous pecan pie after my meatloaf."

"Make that two slices," Sarah quickly added.

Anne nodded. "Meatloaf plate, burger plate, two coffees and two slices of my pecan pie, coming right up," she said. As she walked away, she shoved a lock of her short gray hair back into the tight bun she wore at the nape of her neck. She paused at the kitchen door, drew in a deep breath, and then disappeared through the door. Seconds later the sounds of muffled arguing were heard as Anne gave her husband their orders. No one in the diner batted an eyelash.

"Anne and Wilson fuss at each other all day long, but they'll die in each other's arms before they'll ever spend an hour apart," Amanda said in a dreamy voice. "Forty-two years of marriage and still going."

Sarah stared at the kitchen door. In her mind, she tried to reframe Anne and Wilson's out of sight argument from Amanda's more romantic viewpoint, and visualized the couple making up after their fight with a kiss. She shook her head to clear the strange sight. Her arguments with her own now-ex-husband had never ended quite so romantically. "Love is nice...when you have it," she said somewhat sourly and then quickly looked at Amanda. "I didn't mean...what I meant to say—"

"No, I know," her friend said softly. "Being divorced is the pits," Amanda finished for Sarah.

Sarah nodded. "Yes, it is. I'll say this...what you say about Anne and Wilson never being apart, that's the thing that I miss. I miss...coming home to...love," she sighed. "My cabin is nice and I'm very grateful to live there...but sometimes...at night when the wind is howling...the walls are lonely."

Amanda reached across the table and patted Sarah's hands gently. "You have me, love," she smiled. "I don't want you to feel lonely. If you want, I can spend the night with you tonight. We can make popcorn, watch sappy movies, cry our eyes out, and pass out with chocolate on our breath."

"Oh, but Jack would miss you, June Bug."

Amanda shrugged her shoulders. "My sanity could use a night off."

Sarah considered Amanda's offer but declined. She knew there were some kinds of loneliness that even a best friend couldn't help fix, no matter how much chocolate they brought you. "You belong with your husband, not me."

Amanda sighed. "I belong with my husband, not that bloody bell of his." Amanda threw her chin into the palms of her hands. "The man has a glass of water sitting right next to him on his night stand, but what does he do? He rings that bell of his and summons me to hand him a glass of water that is within arm's reach. Please, Los Angeles, I'm making you this offer not just for you. I need it, too. Let me spend the night with you tonight."

Sarah spotted Anne walking out of the kitchen carrying two white mugs of coffee. "No, my friend. Someday you'll thank me," she promised Amanda.

Amanda sighed again. "Someday my pretty hair is going to fall out," she corrected Sarah and then was distracted by Anne's approach. "Well, at least I'm being treated to a delicious lunch." Amanda sat up straighter in the booth and accepted her cup of coffee from Anne. "Thank you."

Anne handed Sarah her cup of coffee. "Do me a favor," she asked dryly.

"What's that?" Sarah asked and took a sip of her coffee.

"Shoot me," Anne muttered and walked back to the kitchen. When the door swung open to admit her, it disgorged a puff of smoke, the clatter of a spatula against the grill top, and the cacophony of Mr. Wilson Rainy's choice words about his customers' orders on that fine Alaska afternoon. Anne's voice joined her husband's and as the kitchen door swung shut again, their argument rose and fell again under the sounds of a crooning Patsy Cline on the jukebox.

Amanda grinned. Sarah grinned back at her friend. Love sure was grand in the spring.

chapter two

S arah placed a brown shopping bag down onto the kitchen table in her cabin and was debating whether or not to make a fresh pot of coffee when the telephone rang. "Will you grab the phone for me?" she asked Amanda. "I'll make you a cup of coffee for the road."

"I can't believe you're sending me home to that bell," Amanda groaned. She walked over to the telephone hanging beside the refrigerator and snatched it up. "Hello? ...Oh, hello, Andrew...oh, I see...so soon. Sure, sure, we'll be right down." Amanda put down the phone and smiled. "It's a reprieve," she beamed. "It's off to the police station and not home to that bloody bell after all." Amanda began a happy dance around the kitchen. "No bell today."

Sarah rolled her eyes indulgently as she watched her best friend dance around the kitchen. "Okay, silly, grab your purse and let's go."

"Just a second," Amanda said as she dashed over to the telephone and called her husband. "Hi love, this is your wife...no, no time soon, I'm afraid. Los Angeles and I have official police business to take care of down at the police station...don't worry about dinner, I'll have someone from the diner deliver you something...I'm sorry, love, but police business is police business..." Amanda winked happily at Sarah. "I'll be home later...a bit late, I'm afraid. I love you. Bye for now." She hung up.

"Poor Jack."

"Poor Jack, my foot," Amanda huffed. "That man has a mountain of snacks around his bed, the television remote control in hand, enough crosswords to last a century, water bottles everywhere, his walking cane and that silly wheelchair within reaching distance...why, you'd think he suffered a grand trauma instead of a silly broken leg."

"A broken leg is nothing to sneeze at, June Bug."

"Maybe not," Amanda agreed, "but my dear husband is alive and well and will heal up from head to toe. He does not need me waiting on him hand and foot!"

What could Sarah say? She wasn't in Amanda's shoes, dealing with a grumpy husband on the mend. "Coffee for the road?"

"Better make us a thermos full of the good stuff," Amanda encouraged her. "There's no telling what we're going to be dealing with once we arrive at the police station, love."

"A lot of headaches, no doubt," Sarah replied and hurried to make the coffee. Amanda sat down at the kitchen table and waited. As Sarah poured the water into the coffee maker, she turned to Amanda to share with her some of what she had learned. "Peter informed me that Mr. Hopski is...was…a man worth quite a bit of money. If my guess is correct and we have four hungry gold diggers buzzing around Andrew's office, then aside from our public relations work, we really need to focus on the autopsy report. We need to make sure Mr. Hopski's death wasn't foul play."

Amanda studied Sarah's face. Something in her best friend's eyes caught her attention. "Ah, there is something more...much more. Do tell."

Sarah nodded as she scooped fresh, strong coffee into the filter above the coffee pot on the kitchen counter. "All four of

Mr. Hopski's family members hurried up here to our little town. Why? Why didn't they arrange for the deceased...I mean, for Mr. Hopski to be taken back?"

"Thanks for softening the punch, love," Amanda said in a grateful voice. Then she rubbed her chin. "Yes, why didn't they just make arrangements for the poor man to be taken back to Los Angeles? Why did the whole family need to come?"

"That's a very good question, June Bug. Also," Sarah pointed out, "it's required that the State of Alaska perform an autopsy. Apparently when Andrew informed them of this information, someone was not too happy. They wanted the body released right away. With the money Mr. Hopski's family has, they could easily request a second autopsy that could be performed in Los Angeles. It seems to me, and I could be wrong, that Mr. Hopski's 'Eager Beavers' might have some hidden concerns that we need to investigate."

"Oh, I like," Amanda said in a sneaky voice. "I wonder what secrets they're hiding?"

"I'm sure we're going to find out."

"This reminds me of the game Clue," Amanda told Sarah and rubbed her hands together. "I was always very good at that game."

"I'm sure you were," Sarah assured her best friend with a grin. She leaned against the kitchen counter listening to the coffee dripping steadily into the pot and studied Amanda's face. "At least we're not dealing with dangerous killers. At least I don't *think* we are. Even if we aren't, we stay together as a team, right?"

"You bet," Amanda promised. "We learned the hard way that going our separate ways only leads to difficulties and hardships."

Sarah nodded. "We're a team, June Bug. You and me."

"And Conrad," Amanda added with a mischievous wink. Sarah blushed. "Okay, okay, for now, we'll let the topic of love rest and focus on the case at hand." Amanda placed her hands down onto her lap and studiously furrowed her brow in concentration. "So, tell me Detective Garland, love, in your professional opinion, what do you surmise that we are up against?"

Sarah folded her arms together. "We'll know a little more once we get the autopsy report back. From everything Andrew said, it does appear that Mr. Hopski died from exposure to the elements. However, appearances can be deceiving."

Amanda nodded. As she did, a sudden thought rushed into her mind. "Say," she said, her eyes growing wide with fear, "if Mr. Hopski was murdered, you don't suppose the murderer could still be lurking around, do you?"

"Let's not get too worried about that," Sarah reassured her friend, smiling at her flight of fancy. "Andrew said the body of Mr. Hopski appeared to have been dead for a long period of time. If the poor man was murdered, I wouldn't assume his killer would still be around. However," Sarah added, "if he was murdered, I do know where we would start looking: the killer could easily be one of his own family members...or someone else hiding in the shadows. But if that's the case, we will no doubt turn up plenty of clues."

Amanda solemnly nodded. "Okay, Los Angeles, I think my mind is ready to tackle this case."

Sarah glanced down at the coffee pot and drew in a deep breath of the freshly brewed aroma as the coffee started to drip into the pot. For a few moments, she let her mind rest in the cozy aroma and thought about how nice it would be to take a trip down to Los Angeles and see Peter, and maybe even have a picnic on the beach. But her memories of Los Angeles were not sunny, they were clouded by the image of her ex-husband that rushed into her mind, followed by the memories of their very painful divorce. "Me, too, I'm ready for whatever happens," she told Amanda as she turned off the coffee machine and resolutely pushed the image of her ex-husband out of her mind.

"Hey, are you okay?" Amanda asked, alarmed at her friend's sudden grim tone of voice.

Sarah shrugged her shoulders and tried to hide her thoughts by turning to get the coffee thermos out of the cupboard. She reluctantly turned back, turning the metal hulk of the thermos over in her hands, contemplating. "You know...I never would have thought that I would end up divorced and living in Alaska. My marriage...my life, seemed so concrete...so...secure. Of course, when the red flags appeared I simply ignored them." She swallowed the lump in her throat. "Like a fool."

"You're not a fool."

"I was," Sarah said back, sharper than she intended. She looked into Amanda's eyes apologetically. "I didn't act until the iceberg struck my marriage dead on, June Bug. And by then, my marriage was too damaged to save... My ex-husband's heart...his love for me...was gone. Like it had sunk into an icy sea." Sarah sighed. "I blamed myself for the divorce for a long, long time. Now I know it takes two to tango. I didn't force my husband to leave me, he chose to. But why? Why didn't I see the signs that he was pulling away? I was a faithful wife, loyal and dedicated. But I didn't see it. Was I working too many long hours? Was my job too demanding? Was he intimidated by my friends on the force? Did my job not leave enough room for our love to flourish?" Sarah shrugged her shoulders again. "He stopped loving me and there's nothing I can do to change that. All I can do now is go on with my life. But...it hurts."

"I know, love."

Sarah looked down at the coffee pot again. "I wish I could say old wounds have healed, but I would be lying to you. That's why I'm not ready for a relationship. I need time to heal. Of course," Sarah added, "dealing with these murder cases has taken my mind off my troubles. And believe it or not, I'm writing better, too. I finished off my last novel before the snow started to melt. My publisher was very happy."

Amanda stood up, walked over to Sarah, and hugged her. "You're going to be okay, love. And don't worry, we'll never get a divorce." Amanda winked at Sarah. "We're family for life, you and me. And someday, when the time is right, a good man will come into your life."

"Do you really think so?" Sarah asked in a hopeful voice.

"I do," Amanda smiled. She motioned around the kitchen with her eyes. "Someday your cabin might be filled with a grumpy husband ringing a bloody bell."

"I can wait for the bell," Sarah giggled and nudged Amanda with her elbow. "Thanks, June Bug."

Amanda nudged Sarah back. "That's what best friends are for. And speaking of best friends, please, oh please, let me spend the night with you. Jack can live off his pretzels and York Peppermint Patties until I return home."

Sarah started to protest, but then she smiled. Oh, what the heck, she thought. "Sure, June Bug. But I can't stand the idea of our friendship intruding too much on your marriage – it's too close to what sunk my own marriage. So instead of you sleeping here, I'll sleep over at your cabin. Misery does love company."

Amanda cocked her head to one side, considering Sarah's offer. "This does appeal to my poor, aggravated mind. Hey, love, I like the way your mind thinks. We can tackle my husband in shifts."

"I'm sure we can," Sarah agreed. "I'll bring the earmuffs and aspirin."

Amanda broke out laughing. "And I'll tie the hanging noose as a last resort!"

"Speaking of nooses, Andrew might be ready to hang himself by now. He's a good man, but he's not really a people person."

"Poor dear," Amanda agreed. "I guess we better hurry to his rescue."

Sarah studied the coffee pot. "A couple more minutes and we'll be set. In the meantime, I need to use the bathroom."

"I'll mind the kitchen."

Sarah nodded and rushed off. Amanda smiled and sat back down at the kitchen table. She let her eyes roam around the kitchen. The kitchen was warm and cozy and felt like a second home to her. Of course, it was her best friend who made the kitchen feel like a second home. "She deserved better than that bloke who hurt her heart," she fussed to herself. "Poor dear."

The telephone rang again. "Well, this place is like Victoria Station today," she muttered. Amanda stood, walked over to the phone, and answered the call. "Oh, hello Conrad," she said in a pleased voice.

"Hello, Amanda," Conrad said, standing in a smoky office holding a lukewarm cup of coffee in his hand. "How are things in Snow Falls?"

"Oh, the same as always," Amanda smiled. "How are things in New York?"

Conrad looked down at the stale cup of coffee he was holding. "The same," he confessed. "Coffee is still lousy, donuts are still stale and crime is still rampant."

Amanda detected a touch of homesickness in Conrad's voice. "Could it be you're missing the peace and quiet of Alaska?"

"Could be," Conrad confessed. "Is Sarah around?"

"She's...powdering her nose," Amanda told Conrad, looking around to see if Sarah had emerged yet.

"I see," Conrad said. "Listen, Andrew called me and—"

"Oh, that man," Amanda fussed.

Conrad chuckled. He could imagine Amanda's face. "Listen, if you two get into any serious trouble with this case, call me and I'll jump on a flight back home. Andrew doesn't seem to think this Mr. Hopski was murdered, but just in case any funny business did take place—"

"Yes, yes, we'll call you," Amanda promised Conrad. "I'm going to kick Andrew in his knee for bothering you. His bad knee. What does he think Los Angeles and I are, anyway? A couple of helpless women?"

"No, no," Conrad replied hurriedly, jumping into damage control mode. "Amanda, I am Senior Detective and it's Andrew's job to notify me when a body is found. He assured me of the confidence he has in you and Sarah."

"Oh...well, I guess that does make sense," Amanda cooled down and then she kicked herself for being so silly. "Andrew would have to notify you...why didn't I realize that? Silly me."

"Silly you," Conrad agreed, breathing a sigh of relief. "Listen, I better get my nose back to the grindstone. Tell Sarah I called. And if you girls get into any trouble, call me."

"We will," Amanda promised. "Conrad?"

"Yeah?"

"Come home soon, okay? Snow Falls isn't the same without you and a certain person, even though she will never admit it openly, misses you. But you didn't hear that from me." Amanda looked around again hurriedly but luckily there was no sign of Sarah.

"Of course," Conrad assured Amanda. "Oh, by the way, how is Jack's leg? Poor guy took quite a hard fall off your roof."

"Don't get me started on my dear hubby and that bloody bell of his," Amanda said through gritted teeth.

"That bad, huh?"

"Nails down a chalkboard," Amanda confessed.

Conrad nodded and drained his stale coffee in one gulp. The coffee tasted horrible. He missed Sarah's coffee. He missed Sarah. "Broken legs do heal in time," he attempted to comfort Amanda.

"But one's sanity doesn't," Amanda countered.

Conrad laughed. "True," he said.

"Alright, enough chit-chat. Put your eyes back to the sidewalk—"

"Nose back to the grindstone—"

"That, too," Amanda smiled. They said goodbye and she hung up the phone. A minute later, Sarah walked back into the kitchen. "That was Conrad."

"Oh?" Sarah said noncommittally, walking over to pour the coffee into the thermos.

"Apparently Andrew called him?"

"Of course. Since Conrad is the Senior Detective," Sarah said.

Amanda silently cursed herself for being a fool. "I made a big fuss of it, I'm afraid."

"Of course you did," Sarah replied and looked over her shoulder at Amanda and smiled. "Let me guess," she said, "Conrad called to say that if you and I get into any trouble we should call him, right?"

"Yep," Amanda nodded her head. She walked over to Sarah and watched her secure the lid of the thermos. "He cares, you know."

"I know he does."

"He's also very hurt inside, just like you," Amanda pointed out.

"I know."

Amanda stood silent for a few seconds. When she spoke, her voice was soft. "Keep your heart open to him, love."

Sarah looked into Amanda's warm, caring eyes. "I never closed my heart off to begin with," she promised. "Now, we better get our back ends in gear and get down to the police station."

"One sec," Amanda said. She ran over to the refrigerator, snatched the door open, and pulled out a box of day-old cinnamon rolls. "Now we're ready for the road."

Sarah turned off the coffee pot and checked the kitchen. "I'll unpack my sweaters later," she said, glancing briefly at the shopping bag sitting untouched on the kitchen table.

Amanda walked over to the kitchen door and opened it. "Shall we?"

"Away we go," Sarah said. She grabbed the green thermos and walked outside into the fresh air of an Alaska day filled with sunlight that practically sparkled through the limbs of the lush evergreens. She soaked in the beauty as she walked to Amanda's truck. The day was far too beautiful to be spent questioning and babysitting a bunch of selfish – not to mention possibly dangerous – gold-digging eager beavers. She blinked and thought she saw Peter standing beside her Subaru with his fishing pole in hand, grinning at her to hurry up and get moving. "You old grouch," Sarah whispered in a wistful voice, ignoring another lump in her throat. She climbed into the passenger's seat of the truck and closed the door.

Natalie Hopski watched Sarah and Amanda walk into Andrew's stuffy office with cynical, cold eyes. "Where are they?" she demanded without even a greeting.

Sarah quickly examined the older woman before her. She had expected to find the kind of fit, tanned rich woman she used to see everywhere in Los Angeles in her years as a detective there. Instead, she saw that Natalie Hopski was a very large woman with short, abundantly curly – even poufy – auburn hair that was obviously dyed. She wore a purple dress that was as fluffy with chiffon ruffles as her hair was poufy, and the whole effect reminded Sarah rather unfortunately of a clown. But, Sarah cautioned herself, Natalie Hopski's eyes were brilliant and belied the dangerous personality hiding behind this extravagantly strange exterior.

Not wanting to be rude, Sarah extended a hand to Natalie Hopski. Natalie finally shook Sarah's hand perfunctorily, the grip of her large hand firm, if sweaty. "Hello, Ms. Hopski. My name is Detective Garland. I'm acting Detective while Detective Spencer is away. This is my partner, Detective Funnel." Sarah wiped her palm on her jacket and hoped Natalie didn't see.

Amanda offered a quick and professional smile toward Natalie. "We hope your flight went well. And we are so very sorry for the unfortunate loss of your father."

"Yes," Natalie snapped. She focused her attention back on Andrew who was sitting behind his wooden desk, shifting uneasily in his seat. "I want to see my father's body."

"Unfortunately—" Visibly uncomfortable, Andrew began to speak, his eyes begging Sarah's for help.

"Once the state autopsy is completed we'll make the necessary arrangements for a viewing," Sarah spoke smoothly for Andrew. Andrew gave Sarah a grateful look.

Sarah's statement did not please Natalie. "My two brothers and that woman are due to arrive at any moment. I do not like a crowd and I would like to see my father's body in peace," she scolded Sarah. "Is that too much to ask?"

"No, ma'am, it isn't. But we have rules and protocols that must be followed. Your father's body was found dead. State regulations require an official autopsy in order to rule out any foul play."

"In other words, you want to make sure my father wasn't murdered?" Natalie huffed. "The very idea. My father was a very old man." Natalie shook her head. "It's a wonder he didn't drop dead years ago on one of his ill-advised trips to who-knows-where. At times, he would disappear for weeks on one of his hunting trips without telling anyone."

"So, you were unaware that Mr. Hopski traveled to Alaska on a hunting trip?" Sarah asked with an air of mild surprise. The last thing she wanted was for Natalie to suspect that they were already testing avenues of investigation with these questions.

"Of course not. Don't you have ears?" Natalie said indignantly, pursing her lips as if biting back further insults.

Amanda began to loosen her tongue, but Sarah quickly shook her head at her. "Mr. Hopski was an experienced hunter, I take it?"

Natalie nodded her head. "My father hunted every game known to man. His favorite hunting locations are...were...in Africa. But a few years back he became obsessed with hunting bears. Why? Who knows? Sometimes I think that man wanted a bear to kill him."

"Why would you say that?" Sarah asked.

"Because my father was suffering from mental illness," Natalie snapped. "The poor man was never mentally sound from day one. Everyone knew about it. One day he would be in the best of moods and the next he would rip your head off."

"Are you saying he was bi-polar?"

"I see your keen detective's mind is hard at work," Natalie muttered, rolling her eyes.

Sarah ignored the barb. "Did your father take any medication for his depression?"

"I'm not sure. My father was very difficult to handle," Natalie told Sarah and abruptly changed the subject. "Where is the autopsy being performed?" she demanded.

"The autopsy is being performed locally," Andrew informed Natalie. The woman turned to him again, incensed. His wide eyes told Sarah that he had no idea how to cope with the visitor's barrage of rudeness.

"I want to see—"

"When the autopsy is completed we will make the necessary arrangements," Sarah repeated in a firm tone, interrupting the tirade. "Ms. Hopski, please understand. We have to rule out unnatural causes of death. Can you understand that?"

Natalie shot Sarah an icy stare. "I can understand your little backwater town is trying to stop me with a lot of red tape. I won't stand for it. I will call my lawyer if you refuse to grant me permission to see

my—"

"Permission is denied until the autopsy is completed," Sarah interrupted Natalie. She met the woman's glare with a calm demeanor, remembering every suspect she had ever stared down in a police station. "Ms. Hopski, out of respect for Mr. Hopski, I will ensure that every measure is taken to rule out that he was murdered. Once I rule out murder, I will make the arrangements you have requested. Are we clear?"

"We will be," Natalie promised. She stood up, holding her black purse, and walked over to the office door. She looked at Sarah with malice. "I have very delicate business matters to attend to, Detective Garland. If you interfere with me, you'll lose your job. That I guarantee."

"I'm retired," Sarah fired back with mild humor. "As I told you earlier, right now I'm the acting detective until Detective Spencer returns."

Natalie stared at Sarah for a few seconds, then stormed out of the office and slammed the door behind her. "Wow, what a woman," Andrew said in the silence that remained. He stood up and began scratching his legs through the stiffly starched trousers of his uniform. "You ladies have your work cut out for you."

"When will the results of the autopsy come back?" Sarah asked Andrew.

"A couple of days, maybe tomorrow? Depends. This is a small town, Sarah."

Amanda shook her fists at the office door. "Oh, I could just punch her lights out!"

"This is a good lesson for you, Amanda. Never take it

personally," Sarah said. "If you let people like Natalie Hopski get under your skin, you let them take control." Sarah focused back on Andrew. "Where is Ms. Hopski staying?"

"At the lodge in town."

Sarah nodded her head. "I assume that's where Chet and Milton Hopski will be staying, too?"

"Yep," Andrew said. "And Mrs. Hopski, the young wife, too."

"Interesting," Sarah said.

"Why?" Andrew asked.

"My old friend in Los Angeles informed me that Natalie Hopski and Charlene Nelton can't stand to be in the same room together. And now they are staying at the same lodging."

"Well, Snow Falls is a small town," Andrew pointed out. "It's not like they have much choice, and the lodge really is the nicest place."

"If I couldn't stand someone I would find another roof to sleep under, by hook or by crook," Amanda told Andrew. She looked at Sarah. "Are you thinking Clown Woman is in cahoots with Mrs. Gold Digger?"

"Maybe, maybe not," Sarah said and bit down on her lower lip. Before she could continue, she heard an argument erupt from the lobby. "Here we go," she said and rushed out of the office just in time to see a tall, skinny woman pointing one trembling, bony finger at Natalie.

"You killed my husband!" Charlene Nelton screamed at Natalie in a hoarse voice.

"Oh, you little diseased, gold-digging brat," Natalie fired back, advancing on the younger woman with menace, "how dare you accuse me of anything? Who are you to—"

"Just a minute, ladies," Sarah ran up and stood between the two women, "this is a police station, not a wrestling ring."

Charlene looked at Sarah unkindly. Sarah saw that the woman's face was boney, as if half-starved. Even by the standards of image-obsessed Los Angeles, Sarah was immediately struck by something in that face. It was the ugliness of the greed and hunger for power in her eyes. "Who are you?"

"Detective Garland," Sarah introduced herself, offering a friendly handshake as she studied Charlene's hair that had been bleached one too many times and her severe, dark gray dress that was presumably meant to convey power. "Charlene Nelton, I presume?"

"Charlene Hopski," Charlene replied icily, withdrawing from the handshake after barely touching Sarah's hand with her own stiff, bony fingers. "My maiden name is Nelton."

"Your name is still Nelton," Natalie barked at Natalie, trying to push around Sarah. "You gold-digging brat—"

"How dare you!" Charlene practically shrieked with indignation, craning her sinewy neck around to stare daggers at Natalie. "I loved my husband and—"

"Love? Oh, don't make me vomit," Natalie roared back. "You manipulated my father into marrying you."

"How dare you!" Charlene reached out to slap Natalie. Sarah quickly caught her hand and started to try to calm them down once again, but Charlene wasn't having it. "Let go of me," she snapped and viciously yanked her hand away from Sarah.

"Ladies!" Sarah finally shouted in a stern tone that brooked no further interruptions. "Enough. This is a police station. Unless you wish to be booked for public assault, act civil or leave the premises."

The two women, still heaving with pent-up fury, stood stock-still in the lobby as they each waited for the other to leave first. Finally, Natalie backed away a few steps. But she couldn't resist one parting shot.

"You need to be brought down a notch," Natalie warned Sarah. "And I may be just the woman to put you in your place."

"You may leave now," Sarah told Natalie, setting her mouth in a grim line. She pointed at the front door. "At once." She had no more patience for threats, not in her little town, not today, and not ever.

Natalie scowled. "I expect to be contacted with the results of my father's autopsy immediately," she told Sarah and stormed out of the police station.

Charlene rolled her eyes and said snidely, "You should have let me slap her senseless."

"No violence," Sarah warned Charlene.

Charlene drew in a deep breath, patted her hair into place, and smoothed the front of her dress. She turned on an apologetic, simpering smile that made Sarah's skin crawl, even though she knew this was simply a calculated act. "I would like to see my husband's body now."

Sarah shook her head. "I'm afraid that's simply not possible yet. When the official autopsy is completed, I will make the arrangements for a viewing. Until then, we must ask for your patience and understanding."

Charlene folded her arms together, the fake smile leaving her face. "Can I at least gather my husband's belongings?"

"Not yet," Sarah said without apology. "This is an investigation and his belongings are evidence."

"Evidence? An investigation?" Charlene asked, wrinkling her nose in distaste. "It was made clear to me that my husband died from exposure."

"Possibly," Sarah explained. "But we must rule out other possibilities, as well."

"You mean murder?" Charlene asked in an acidic tone. The way her eyes stared out from the bony hollows of her face, a look of withering disdain, was enough to make a flower wilt.

"Yes."

"Oh please, who would want to murder my husband? My husband was adored by everyone," Charlene rolled her eyes.

"Detective, you're barking up the wrong tree if you believe—"

"Every possibility must be ruled out," Sarah repeated firmly. "We ask for your patience. Please accept my sincere condolences for the loss of your husband."

An expression of grief came over Charlene's face as if cued by the mention of her loss. "Yes, I was devastated when I was informed about my husband's death. I began asking myself a million questions..." Charlene took a lace handkerchief out of her purse and sniffed as if some tears would fall, but Sarah couldn't help but see that her eyes remained perfectly dry.

"Did Mr. Hopski tell you he was traveling to Alaska on a hunting trip?" Sarah asked Charlene.

Charlene shook her head no. "My dear husband never told anyone when he went hunting. He would just simply vanish overnight, guns and jackets packed up and his closet a mess." Charlene wiped at her eyes. "My husband was older than me, of course. He made his fortune and he liked living a certain way, so I never felt that it was my place to ask him about his hunting trips or complain when he would just up and leave."

Sarah nodded. "Did your husband take medication for his depression?"

Charlene's face went from sad to stony in a split second. "Is that what that bag of fat told you?" she spit out between tightly pressed lips.

Sarah saw out of the corner of her eye as Amanda clamped one hand over her mouth to stifle a helpless laugh and then ran back toward Andrew's office. Andrew quickly followed her, leaving Sarah in the lobby with Charlene. Sarah summoned every ounce of professionalism to keep a straight face. "Uh, yes. I do believe she – Ms. Hopski mentioned that."

Charlene fumed. "My husband did not suffer from depression, Detective," she snapped. "My husband may have been older than me, and he certainly had his moods, but his mind was sharp and brilliant. He was certainly not mentally ill, no matter what you might hear from his ungrateful children," she spat out.

"I see," Sarah finally said, reserving her thoughts. "Well, the autopsy report will tell us if your husband had any medication in his system."

Charlene quickly glanced down at her feet and then back up at Sarah. "Well, if my husband was on any medication for depression, I wasn't aware of it."

"I would have thought a wife would know about her husband's medical issues," Sarah queried.

"Are you trying to suggest that I was a bad wife?" she fired back.

"No," Sarah said in a calm voice, "I'm stating that if you are lying to me, the autopsy will show it."

"How dare you suggest—!"

"You may leave now, too," Sarah said and pointed at the front door. "I'll be in touch."

"You better be," Charlene demanded. "I'm staying at—"

"I'm aware," Sarah assured Charlene, ushering her firmly toward the door.

Charlene stopped at the threshold, holding the handle of the lobby door, and stared at Sarah. Sarah wasn't the type of woman you wanted to match wits with. However, Charlene drew herself up to her full height, even though she wavered like a twig on her too-high heels. She was a spoiled young woman, used to getting everything she wanted. "Maybe you do need to be brought down a notch," she said in a snide undertone. "As if this town isn't low enough as it is."

"You may leave," Sarah said in a tougher tone.

Charlene rolled her eyes at Sarah. "Whatever, I'm out of here," she said and walked out the door.

Sarah walked over to the front door, looked out the nearby window, and watched Charlene march up to a flashy red BMW, jump into the front seat and speed away. She spotted

Natalie sitting across the street in a black Lincoln Town Car. Natalie drove away as soon as Charlene was down the road. "Interesting," Sarah said, and walked back to Andrew's office. "You two," she said and rolled her eyes at her friends.

"Bag of fat?" Andrew burst out laughing again. Amanda joined in. "Oh, wait till the wife hears about that one!"

Amanda slapped her knee. "I thought I was going to die laughing! It's like the circus is in town. Oh my, I can't breathe."

Sarah shook her head and grinned. She leaned back against the office door and waited for her friends to laugh it out. "Well, that Laurel and Hardy nightmare pair might seem like a laughing matter, but they need to be taken seriously."

Amanda tried to stop laughing but couldn't. Andrew wiped tears from his eyes. "My side hurts," he said and grabbed his ribs. "Who knew Los Angeles folk talked like that?"

"Alright, you two," Sarah said, "let's try to focus." But as soon as she said those words, Amanda made a face and gestured with her hands in a pouf above her head, mimicking Natalie's outrageous hair, and Sarah burst out laughing herself. "I guess it was kinda funny."

"A real female Laurel and Hardy," Amanda laughed.

"The circus is definitely in town," Andrew laughed even harder. They all doubled up anew.

Even Sarah laughed until it hurt, and then finally took a calming breath. "Okay," she said and wiped tears from her eyes, "we need to focus—"

Before Sarah could finish her sentence, the door to the office burst open and a short man with a comically round, portly belly appeared, wearing an expensive-looking but rumpled gray, pinstriped suit and a gray fedora that had seen better days. He had the chewed-up end of a fat cigar in his mouth and a face that looked like a prize fighter after a heavyweight title match – rough, wary, but used to winning.

He snatched the cigar end from his mouth as he looked the three of them up and down quickly. "My name is Milton Hopski. Which one of you is in charge?"

Andrew took one look at Milton and bolted up from his chair and left the office. Amanda took off after him. "You'll have to excuse my friends, they, uh, have important work to take care of," Sarah told Milton as she bit back the laugh that she knew her friends were hiding in the hall to let out. "Please, come in. My name is Detective Garland. I'm the acting detective until Detective Spencer returns from New York."

Milton stepped further into Andrew's office so that his bulk blocked the door. He took a slow, appraising look at Sarah and smiled. "Say, detective, maybe you and I can have dinner tonight. It sure is cold up here in Alaska, but I like it hot." Milton tossed Sarah a flirty wink.

"Oh my," Sarah whispered and hurried to put Andrew's desk between them before he could approach any nearer. Milton's smile widened as he started chatting up the pretty female detective.

Far away in New York City, Conrad poured himself a cup of coffee and began wondering how Sarah was making out back home. "I'm sure she's doing fine," he told himself, not realizing that at that very moment, Milton Hopski was scheming to make Sarah his sixth wife.

chapter three

Milton Hopski eased toward Andrew's desk. "Now, don't be shy," he coaxed Sarah and patted one of the brown chairs in front of the desk. "Come and sit down by Milton and let's talk."

Sarah couldn't believe her eyes. This strange little man with a round stomach sticking out from the rumpled jacket of his mobster suit was flirting with her. Good grief. Spring usually brought strange, randy creatures out of the hills in a normal year, but strange people? This took the cake, she thought to herself. "Mr. Hopski—"

"Please, call me Milton, hot stuff. And might I add, that dress you're wearing...*rawr*," Milton made a flirty growling sound and winked at Sarah again.

"Uh...thank you," Sarah said, wondering how she was going to deal with the wolf standing before her. "Mr. Hopski —Milton, on behalf of the city of Snow Falls, please accept our deepest condolences to you and your family for your loss."

Milton shrugged his shoulders and tossed one hand in dismissal. "My old man was older than the hills, babe. It was only a matter of time before he kicked the bucket, eh?"

"Uh, yes, I suppose," Sarah agreed. "Still, a tragic ending."

Chastened, Milton pulled a sad face and took the fedora hat off, revealing a nearly bald head. A few stringy gray hairs stood here and there like lost soldiers. "My old man lived a long life. Now he's taken his last voyage. That's the way of things," Milton told Sarah with a shrug of his shoulders, popping his hat back on his head.

She thought of the elderly man's last moments on the frozen mountain, and the terrible cold that must have enveloped him. She shivered a little, glad that the dark winter had at last passed into spring, even if it had brought the Hopskis to Snow Falls. "God is the beginning and the end of all things and all men, Mr. Hopski. Death is not to be taken lightly."

Milton stared at Sarah. "Say, you're okay," he smiled.

Sarah could tell that Milton wasn't a bad guy – confused and eccentric, yes; but not bad. In fact, the man was oddly charming in his old-fashioned mannerisms, if she ignored his over-the-top flirting. She smiled. "Thanks."

"So, what about that dinner, huh? Let me take you out, Detective."

"Uh...sorry," Sarah replied, amused by his sudden shift back to flirting. "You're very nice to offer, but I'm recently divorced and kinda licking my wounds right now."

"I've been dropped by five wives. Take it from an expert: in time, you'll grow numb," Milton explained. "Best way to get over being dropped is to get right back in the saddle, too," he winked.

Sarah smiled. Milton was a persistent little fellow. "I'll remember that. In the meantime, I am still the acting detective on this case and will need to ask you a few questions."

"Anything for you, doll." Milton plopped down in a chair. "Fire away."

Sarah eased down into Andrew's desk chair. "Did your father, the older Mr. Hopski, suffer from depression?"

"Pop?" Milton asked and then laughed. "Pop was a prime

candidate for the looney farm. No disrespect intended. If you didn't learn Pop's moods you were in for some hard hits. But hey, Pop was one of a kind. Sure, he was moody, but he was brilliant and clever. He knew when to buy up the land and he made a sweet profit from it, every time. And he sold so many of those lousy mansions to the rich and famous…more like the 'Spoiled and Rotten' if you ask me. Pop knew how to play people like a fiddle and make a pretty penny in the process."

Sarah nodded her head as she took down a few quick notes on the paper in front of her. "And Mr. Hopski also was a skilled hunter, from what I was told?"

Milton twirled the fedora hat on his right finger, lost in a memory. "Pop used to say he could pick off a gazelle at five hundred meters without blinking an eye," he said in a proud voice. "Pop fought the Germans in World War II, you know." Milton stopped twirling the fedora hat and his smile dropped from his face. "I think it was the war that messed with his brain, you know. Before my mother died she told me a lot of stories about Pop and the war."

Sarah studied Milton's face. The man was sincere. "I'm listening."

Milton shrugged his shoulders. "Pop went through some hard battles with his platoon and they were pretty close calls. During one bad firefight, he ended up taking a shot in the gut. Ma said he wouldn't talk about exactly how it happened, but one of his buddies said that he was trying to save someone's life that day. Until he got shot, that is. Anyway, they barely got him out to a field hospital in time to save his life. He lived, of course, but after that his days as a soldier were over. My Ma knew him a little before the war, too, and she always said that he came back a little different. It wasn't just the scar on his stomach – he had scars in his mind, too. 'Too many scars to count,' she always said."

Sarah made a few notes about Milton's story before she continued. "Do you believe it's possible that your father, such an experienced hunter, became lost and died from exposure?" she asked Milton in a careful voice.

"What else could it have been?" He paused and looked at her. "You're asking me if I believe my old man was murdered, right, doll face?" He grimaced.

"Well, yes," Sarah said.

"Because that explains why all of Pop's kids and that wife of his raced up here to claim the body, right? To get his money, right? And," Milton added, a little agitated, "you're probably thinking one of us – if not all of us – are involved in Pop's death somehow." He took a breath and stared down at his hands.

"Possibly."

"Hey, if I were in your shoes I'd be sticking my belly under the hot bulb, too," Milton smiled apologetically at Sarah. "It's pretty obvious that there's some gold diggers among us, including me. I want Pop's money...well, some of it, at least. But not for the reason you think."

"Oh?" Sarah asked.

Milton relaxed and leaned back in the chair. "Pop lined me up real nice through the years. I get twenty thousand a month to live off of...for life. I live a very comfortable life. Let's just say money isn't an issue, hot stuff."

Sarah smiled a little. Being called 'hot stuff' amused her. "Then why do you want your father's money?"

"Because Pop deserves better," Milton said in a serious voice. His face became stern as he leaned in closer. "Listen and listen close, okay?"

"Okay."

"This ain't common knowledge, doll. You have to know this, though. Natalie, Chet and me, we're all adopted. Ma and Pop could never have any natural kids. But not one time did that man ever treat us like charity cases – we were his true children in every way. Pop spoiled every last one of us kids to no end." Milton's smile then faded and he shook his head in disgust. "But Natalie, that woman...she never loved Pop the way we boys did. I don't know why, but she's been like that since she was a little kid. She always ran her mouth, never satisfied, never happy. And when she grew up she had not a single good word to say about him and did everything in her power to hurt him. Even with all the money and support he lavished on her, on all of us! She played with his moods, too. It was like a game for her, seeing how she could hurt him, and what she could get out of it. Usually money. If it wasn't for Chet and me, Pop would have taken some hard hits because of her vendetta. And now that Pop's gone, Chet and me are going to make sure Natalie doesn't get a dollar more, not one red cent. We can't stop her from getting her money from the trust Pop set up for her, the one that pays out monthly, but we can sure sue to get her out of the will."

"You and your brother Chet are close, I take it?"

"Like this," Milton said and crossed his fingers together. "Chet and I have always had each other's backs."

"But you both disliked your father's wife, right?" Sarah asked. "Your stepmother, technically?"

Milton leaned back in his chair. "I never called her that once in my life. Charlene is a backstabbing, ugly soul trapped in a scrawny twig body that ought to be snapped in half. She doesn't deserve to be in the will any more than Natalie does."

Sarah could see the pain written clearly on his face. "Why did your father marry her?"

"Out of a sense of duty," Milton explained. "You see, Pop served with Charlene's grandfather during the war. The two of them were real buddies, you know." Milton shook his head. "Pop always had a tender heart even though he was moody as a cat in a mud puddle. Anyhow, when Pop's buddy died, Pop made a promise to watch after his son."

"Mr. Nelton, the grocery store owner."

Milton nodded his head. "Pop's buddy started the original grocery store and his son took the ball and ran with it. He's a nice enough guy, I guess. A little too Country Club for my taste, but that's none of my business."

"So how did he go from watching over Mr. Nelton to marrying Mr. Nelton's daughter? I can't believe that many fathers would have approved of that marriage. She must have been less than half his age. Did Mr. Nelton approve?"

"No way," Milton burst out. "Like I said, the man is hungry for the good life, but he's decent enough. He was against Charlene marrying Pop from the beginning. But Charlene, that money hungry tick, lied to Pop."

"How so?"

Milton looked over his shoulder and then focused back on Sarah's pretty face. "She made him believe that marriage was the only way to support the granddaughter of his war buddy, if you can believe that. She told Pop that Mr. Nelton was dying of cancer and was leaving all of his money to some charity for animals."

"And Mr. Hopski believed her?"

"Why wouldn't he? Unfortunately, Charlene and her old man were always at each other's throats. Like nothing you've ever seen, doll face. It's likely the man was planning to cut his daughter out of his will, who knows, but she had her sob story ready to go and Pop was taken in, hook, line and sinker. Pop was tied to that promise he made to his old war buddy and decided he had to uphold that promise by marrying Charlene."

Sarah shook her head, trying to comprehend the crazy lives of these rich people. "Why didn't your father simply create a monthly trust fund for her?"

"Because," Milton said in a disgusted tone, "they were in love. Or so he thought. You see, Charlene greased Pop with romance and lies," he told Sarah. "You have to keep in mind, Pop was moody. One day he could be the nicest guy in the world, the next a big cry baby and the next day meaner than a bear. Charlene worked her way into his life on the days

Pop's emotions were vulnerable." He shook his head in resignation.

Sarah folded her arms. "I see," she said. "Natalie and Charlene were in here earlier. Seems like they don't like each other, either."

Milton's hard face relaxed. He grinned. "That's the card those two cats are playing. I know better," he said, tapping one finger on his temple.

Sarah realized she was liking Milton more by the minute. "But why? Do you think they are working together to steal your father's money?"

"Yeah, I do, doll face. And then, when Pop's money is grabbed up, those two cats will probably go twelve rounds with each other and come out bloodier than a butcher shop." Milton tossed a thumb at the office door. "After all, doll face, who do you think taught Charlene how to play Pop like a fiddle?"

Sarah looked at the office door, thinking. "Milton, maybe we will have dinner one night," she smiled.

He winked at her and smiled a little sadly. "But as friends, right? No romance?"

"Sorry," Sarah smiled at Milton.

"Hey, doll face, friends with a diamond like yourself is better than getting a piece of hard coal dropped in the old boiler." Milton stood up. "Chet wasn't too far behind me getting into town. I know he'll want to talk to you alone. And," Milton stretched his arms, "I'm ready for a few winks. I'm staying at your local lodge, doll face. Give me a call when Pop's autopsy report comes back and whatever you do, do me a favor. Don't give out the results to Natalie and Charlene without me and Chet present."

"Deal," Sarah agreed. She stood up and walked Milton to the office door with a smile. "There's a diner down the street that has good food."

Milton donned his fedora hat and rubbed his belly

greedily. "A little grub before a nap wouldn't hurt." He winked at Sarah one last time as he left the office.

Seconds later, Andrew and Amanda peeked around the door and then sheepishly came back in. "You two should be ashamed of yourselves," Sarah scolded her friends.

"So, what did Al Capone have to say?" Andrew said with a chuckle. But he couldn't suppress his laughter, and then Amanda joined in.

"Al Capone...good one," Amanda clapped Andrew on the shoulder. "Oh dear...wait until my hubby hears about this."

Sarah couldn't hold back her smile. Milton did resemble a little mobster, she had to admit. "Well, as it turns out, he's actually quite a nice, normal guy, once you get to know him."

"Truly?" Andrew asked and tried to dry up his laughter. "Oh, well. I thought he'd never leave."

Sarah sighed, wondering how to convey the wealth of information she had just learned from Milton. She shook her head just as the office door opened and Chet Hopski appeared. This time she did not wait and ushered Andrew and Amanda unceremoniously out the door as she greeted the newest visitor. "Mr. Chet Hopski?"

A tall man wearing a gray and blue striped suit stepped into the office, ducking his head a little. The poor man was so tall he barely fit through the door frame. Like his adopted brother, he too had a portly stomach, but he was so tall that his bulk seemed to be spread out all over. Chet was not a handsome man. His face was pale and very jowly, with a deep double chin, and the unfortunate gray toupee that sat slightly crooked on his head didn't help matters any. Yet, Sarah saw intelligence – a brilliant intelligence – in the man's sharp, dark blue eyes; an intelligence hidden from a judgmental world. "Detective Garland?" he asked in a dull, almost slow voice that held none of the comical wit she had heard from Milton. "Nice to meet you." They shook hands briefly.

"Yes," Sarah said and smiled. "Please, Mr. Hopski, sit down."

"I'll stand," Chet said dryly, shifting uncomfortably on his feet. "I met my brother outside. I'm about to join him for a bite to eat. I wanted to introduce myself first."

"I'm very sorry for your loss, Mr. Hopski."

"Thank you," Chet acknowledged, his dry voice not betraying much emotion. "Daddy lived a long life. I'm just grateful his body was found so he can have a decent Christian burial back home."

Sarah nodded her head. "Of course. Mr. Hopski, do you mind if I ask you a couple of questions before you go?"

"Of course. That's your job."

"Do you believe your father was killed?" Sarah cut right to the chase.

"It's possible," Chet nodded his head and then withdrew a gray handkerchief from the right pocket of his jacket and blew his nose with a dry honking sound. "Natalie and Charlene have wanted Daddy dead for a long time."

"And you think they may be behind Mr. Hopski's death?"

"Daddy was a good hunter. He wouldn't have gotten himself lost in the woods," Chet replied and returned the handkerchief to his pocket. "Daddy was a good hunter," he said again. Chet looked down at his feet with sad eyes. "Daddy didn't ever get lost in the woods."

"I see," Sarah said. "Mr. Hopski, is your wife with you?"

Chet shook his head no. "Teresa stayed in Los Angeles." Chet raised his eyes and looked at Sarah. "Teresa doesn't like to fly. Teresa doesn't like dealing with airplanes, you know." He shifted on his feet. "She's...you know...large, like me. On airplanes, people can be so insensitive, insulting you when they think you can't hear. Or even when you can. Like my late father's wife." He looked out the window as if checking to see if perhaps Charlene was listening in on his confession.

"I'm so sorry, Mr. Hopski," Sarah told Chet. "People can

be so cruel and mean. It's especially cruel to have to suffer that treatment from your own stepmother. It's love that matters the most. If you and your wife love each other, then that makes you both the richest people in the world."

Chet nodded his head. Even though his face remained impassive, his eyes smiled. "I'm very blessed," he admitted. "Well, I better go. Milton is waiting for me."

Sarah smiled, feeling an immediate affection for Chet. "I'll be in touch, Mr. Hopski. Please, enjoy your meal."

"I will," Chet said and turned to go. He paused at the office door and looked back at Sarah. "You were a good cop in Los Angeles," he said simply. "I read about you." There was that smile of recognition in his eyes again. Then he ducked through the doorway again and left.

"So, he knows who I am," Sarah smiled in surprise.

When Andrew and Amanda stuck their heads back in the office, Sarah pointed her finger at them. "You two."

Andrew cleared his throat. "Yes, I...uh, not very professional."

"Sorry, partner," Amanda quickly apologized. "So, what did Mr. Big and Tall have to say about—" Amanda couldn't finish her joke. She broke out laughing. Andrew bit down on his lower lip and then joined in.

"While you two were busy being juvenile, I learned some interesting information from Chet Hopski, who seems to be a very decent man," Sarah scolded Amanda and Andrew. "I'm going to go make some copies. And I'm making a report to Conrad about your unprofessionalism, Andrew." As she exited the office with her case file, Andrew sputtered and followed her into the hall, trying to excuse his behavior again.

"Oh dear, what a day," Amanda said as she leaned against the wall in the hallway, watching Andrew following Sarah down the hall like a puppy with his tail between his legs.

"So, what's the plan?" Andrew asked Sarah after they had all returned to the office. He sat down in his chair and waited for Sarah as she reviewed her notes quickly. Outside, a soft and gentle rain began to fall, drifting into a beautiful spring evening.

Sarah listened to the rain fall and gathered her thoughts before speaking. Amanda sat down next to her, taking a bite from her candy bar. "For starters, I need some coffee. Do you have any cups?" Sarah spoke and pointed at the green thermos she had taken out of her bag and perched on the edge of Andrew's desk.

"Sure," Andrew smiled. "Let me go down the hall and get some cups."

Sarah waited until Andrew left the office before speaking. She turned to Amanda and looked at her friend demolishing the candy bar. "I believe our bad guys are Natalie and Charlene. But something tells me, deep down in my gut, there could be more people lurking in the shadows."

"So the midget and fat man...I mean, Milton and Chet...are in the clear, then?" Sarah nodded as Amanda polished off the candy bar. She tossed the wrapper in a trash can beside Andrew's desk. "Nothing like some chocolate to make a woman feel ready to tackle a problem," she said with satisfaction. Amanda walked over to the office window, pulled the blinds to one side, and peeked out into the rain. "Lovely."

Sarah listened to the rain fall. She felt its beauty as if she was in it, with the rain droplets falling through lush, green tree limbs, landing on the rich loamy soil that was slowly defrosting after the long, harsh, winter. She only hoped that this case would resolve itself soon so she could get back to enjoying the delicate beauty of the Alaska spring. She turned to Amanda. "June Bug, I know Natalie Hopski and Charlene Nelton look like a couple of circus rejects – and they fight like a couple of wet cats – but they are dangerous. Both of those women are after Mr. Hopski's fortune and for all we know they might be willing to kill to achieve their goal."

Amanda turned away from the window and looked at her best friend. "I had a bad feeling you were going to say those very words, love," she said and shook her head. "I admit that Natalie Hopski put a sour taste in my mouth."

Sarah nodded her head. "We'll have to wait until we can question her further. Meanwhile, from what I learned, Mr. Hopski fought in World War II." Sarah rubbed her chin. "He may have been traumatized by it, according to Milton, but the main point is that the poor man did fight in the war and gained valuable skills and experience that helped him become an expert hunter. He wasn't just some rich man who liked to go traipsing into the wilderness with a gun."

"What you're trying to relay to me, love, is that you don't think the old man accidentally got lost in the woods and froze to death," Amanda said.

"It's looking less and less likely." Sarah thought back to her conversations as she skimmed her notes again. "Andrew stated that the body...I mean, Mr. Hopski—"

"Thank you, love."

"—Mr. Hopski was found lying in a manner that appeared to indicate that he became lost and froze to death," Sarah continued. "An empty canteen, an empty pack of jerky, all evidence that would point to a person who had consumed their resources while trying to find their way back somewhere. Surely no skilled hunter would travel with just a packet of jerky. He must have been trying to find his way back to a camp. Which leads me to wonder, where was he camped?"

"Ah," Amanda said, "now there is a great question! I'm learning from a very brilliant detective."

"I'm not brilliant," Sarah assured Amanda in a humble voice. "A good detective will simply utilize logic and the process of elimination to make practical conclusions."

"Modest, too," Amanda grinned. "Love, you caught a deadly serial killer while you worked the streets in Los Angeles."

Sarah blushed. "Having some brains helps," she admitted and stood up to hide her embarrassment. "June Bug, I need to know more before I can draw any definite conclusions, but my gut is telling me the man was murdered, which makes me wonder about his will."

"Ah, another good question," Amanda mused. "And this little London gal is wondering if Mr. Hopski's will might have some type of clause in it stating that if he was murdered his fortune would not go to his wife or three children?"

"Now who is the brilliant one?" Sarah asked, turning to gape at Amanda's insight.

Amanda felt her cheeks turn red. "Well, it was only a thought."

"Modest, too."

"Stop it," Amanda told Sarah and blushed even redder.

Andrew returned carrying three brown paper cups. "Okay," he said, "here are the cups."

"I'll pour," Amanda told Andrew and took the three cups from him. "You've been itching like a dog infested with fleas all day. One scratch while pouring coffee and you're likely to burn yourself and spoil Sarah's best brewed coffee, too."

Andrew scratched at his legs again. "Darn starch," he complained. "From now on I'm going to let my wife iron my uniform." Andrew looked at Sarah, who had crossed over to examine a map of the area that hung on his office wall. "Okay, Sarah, talk to me. What are you thinking?"

"I'm wondering, where was Mr. Hopski's campsite located?" Sarah asked Andrew. "Or more likely, where is the poor man's hunting cabin? Surely he was too rich for a mere tent in the woods."

Andrew leaned against his desk. "We haven't located Mr. Hopski's hunting cabin yet," Andrew confessed. "I figured you'd get around to asking me about that sooner or later. Truth be told, Mr. Hopski was found pretty far out, Sarah. His body wouldn't have even been spotted if the folks hadn't wandered off the trail a bit to search for a certain type of bird."

"How far out were they, anyway?" Sarah asked.

"Far enough to make the moose feel lonely," Andrew assured Sarah. "The old Snow Bear Trail shoots straight north through that little valley you see there on the map, and eventually the trail fades off into the land. The trail was created by the native Alaskans who lived and hunted in this area forever, though nowadays it's mainly used by moose and birdwatchers."

"How far down the trail, Andrew? I need a mile count," Sarah asked again, examining the map closely.

"Oh, I'd say...seven or eight miles north from the trailhead. The bird watching group that found Mr. Hopski's body was being driven down the trail by Burt Sterry's boy. Burt Sterry bought his boy an old truck last year and it seems like the boy raised it up on a four-by-four kit and found a way to make a few extra dollars in the backcountry."

"I see," Sarah said. "Did you get the names of everyone in that group?"

"Five locals I have known for years," Andrew assured Sarah. "Not a killer among them, unless you want to consider Mrs. Aspen's cooking a threat against humanity." Andrew smiled. "Poor Mrs. Aspen, the poor thing can't cook to save her life, but she sure tries."

"Mrs. Aspen, the old lady who lives out on Willow Whisper Road?" Sarah asked.

"The very same," Andrew answered. "Mrs. Aspen lives alone in her little cottage. Story goes that after her husband was killed in a car crash she moved to Alaska and secluded herself from the world. She comes out of hiding during the spring to go bird watching with her four widow friends. Burt

Sterry's boy shovels snow for them during the winter, so they trust him well enough."

"I see," Sarah nodded her head. "I'd like to speak to Mrs. Aspen, Mr. Sterry's son, and the other four women who were out bird watching."

Andrew furrowed his brow in concern. "Sarah, Mrs. Aspen is very...delicate. She doesn't speak to just anyone. And that goes for Mrs. Cohen, Mrs. Grifton, Mrs. Daffle and Mrs. Polly. All five women are in their late sixties, Sarah, and they're not interested in speaking to a stranger. I've known Mrs. Aspen for a long time and it took me just about as long to earn her trust. I guess I knew I had earned her trust when she presented me with a burned casserole."

"I bumped into Mrs. Aspen at the grocery store," Amanda chimed in, trying to help Andrew. "I tried to say hello, but received an icy shoulder instead."

"I promise you," Andrew said kindly, "if all other avenues turn up empty, I'll go out and question Mrs. Aspen myself."

Sarah understood. She didn't press the issue. "What about Mr. Sterry's son?"

"Burt Jr. is a good kid. He'll talk to you," Andrew said in a relieved voice. "But I'm not sure what information you're fishing for from the boy, Sarah. Burt Jr. told me everything that happened." Andrew scratched at his legs again. "He was driving Mrs. Aspen and her friends down the old trail in his truck. The five old ladies were sitting in the bed of the truck with their binoculars, bird watching, when Mrs. Aspen tapped the driver's side door with her cane. Burt Jr. said he stopped the truck and helped Mrs. Aspen and her friends down out of the bed and watched them wander off-trail a little in search of some bird. They told him not to follow because they thought his boots would be too loud, you know how young fellas are. Well, a few minutes later he heard Mrs. Daffle scream and went running with his rifle in hand."

"Burt Jr. is a good kid," Amanda pointed out. "Mr. Sterry

and I chatted about him a couple times. He works at the grocery store a couple nights a week to put money away for college. He should be a senior when school starts back, right, Andrew?"

"Yep," Andrew nodded. "Burt Jr. wants to join the Coast Guard, too. I think the kid is going to be okay. He comes from good stock."

Sarah rummaged through her mind and managed to find Burt Jr. "Red headed kid...kinda skinny...friendly smile?"

"That's the kid," Andrew confirmed.

"I remember him now. He carried groceries to my Subaru for me a few times," Sarah explained. She bit down on her lip. "Okay, so Burt Jr. heard Mrs. Daffle scream and went running. What then?"

Andrew accepted a cup of coffee from Amanda and took a careful sip. "Well, Mrs. Aspen and her friends were standing under a large tree. Burt Jr. said when he got to them he saw them looking down at a man lying face up...dead." Andrew took another sip of coffee. "Burt Jr. hurried the women back to his truck and made tracks back toward town."

"Nobody touched the body...nobody touched Mr. Hopski, I mean?" Sarah asked.

Andrew shook his head no. "Burt Jr. said one look was all it took to let him know Mr. Hopski was long dead and he sure wasn't interested in messing with a dead body." Andrew took a third sip of coffee. "Sarah, you have to drive nine miles due north just to reach the old Snow Bear Trail. So, we're talking a pretty good distance from town."

Sarah nodded her head and focused on a different question. "So, Mr. Hopski's cabin is most likely within walking distance of the trail?"

"Must be," Amanda said and handed Sarah a cup of coffee. "If his body...I mean, if Mr. Hopski...was found close to the trail, perhaps he was trying to use the trail to find his way back to civilization."

"Assuming he was even lost," Sarah pointed out and sipped on her coffee. The coffee was very strong and the aroma blended in beautifully with the cozy sound of the pelting rain outside. "What if he was being chased and needed a safe route out of the wilderness?"

"There were no signs the man was attacked, Sarah," Andrew pointed out.

"Maybe not physically," Sarah pointed out. "But he could have been fleeing. Slowly, given his age and the snow in that season. Maybe Mr. Hopski was scared to death."

Andrew stopped sipping his coffee. His ears perked up. "Scared to death?"

Amanda took a slow sip of coffee. Her imagination created a hideous creature with red glowing eyes lurking out in the snow, stalking poor Mr. Hopski, watching...waiting...and then...pouncing on the man with a horrible scream, causing Mr. Hopski's heart to stop with fear. She shivered. "Creepy."

"I guess we'll have to wait to see if it was a heart attack that took him, when the coroner's report comes back. Personally, I wouldn't put it past Natalie Hopski to try to scare her old man to death. Peter did warn me that she is clever," Sarah explained. "The woman may look like a clown, but her eyes are cold and deadly. The same applies to Charlene Nelton. Although," Sarah added, "according to Peter, Charlene isn't as clever as Natalie. Milton backs that up. From what he told me, Charlene is a follower, not a leader, although she may believe she's the smartest cookie in the jar."

"Scared to death...well, I'll be," Andrew whispered to himself as his mind connected the dots Sarah was presenting to him. "I never would have thought..."

Sarah sipped at her coffee. "Let's not get ahead of ourselves. Andrew, it's too late for you to take Amanda and myself to the spot where Mr. Hopski was found. But first thing in the morning, we need you to pick us up at Amanda's cabin. We're going to spend the day searching for Mr. Hopski's hunting cabin."

"I'm a step ahead of you there, Sarah. I called Jessica down at the realty office. She sent me a list of names of everyone who rented seasonal cabins from her. Unfortunately, Mr. Hopski's name isn't on the list."

"Which might mean he owns property in Snow Falls, right?" Amanda asked.

"The land around the trail is protected. No one can build on the land," Andrew explained. He looked at Sarah. "You're wondering about Mr. Hopski's vehicle, too, aren't you?"

"Well, a man his age certainly didn't walk here on foot," Sarah replied and finished her coffee. "It seems, guys, we have a lot of loose ends that need to be tied up."

Andrew nodded his head. "I agree," he stated, grateful Sarah was on board. The woman had presented questions to him he himself never considered. "It seems like maybe...just maybe...we have a murder on our hands."

"And the murderer, or murderers," Amanda said in a careful tone, "could be right here in Snow Falls." Amanda took a sip of her coffee and winced. Her best friend sure knew how to make a strong cup of coffee.

Sarah stood up and walked over to the office window and pulled back the vertical blinds. The soft rain was falling gently over Snow Falls; lazy and relaxed. But somewhere beyond the rain, a dark storm was raging in the Hopski family. "I have a bad feeling about this," Sarah whispered.

Amanda looked at Andrew. Andrew scratched at his leg absently. "Well," he said and looked down at the phone on his desk, "I better start scheduling constant patrols around the lodge so we can keep an eye on our guests."

"Good idea," Sarah agreed. She turned away from the window and looked at Sarah. "Hungry?"

"Starving."

"Let's go get some dinner at the diner," Sarah replied. "Andrew, what would you like for us to bring you back?"

"Oh, a meatloaf plate will do," Andrew said in a grateful voice.

"Sure thing. In the meantime, can one of your deputies find out if Mr. Hopski's rifle has been recently fired?" Andrew agreed and spoke to one of his men as they exited, hungry.

Sarah grabbed Amanda's hand as they headed for the door. "Let's go have dinner with Milton and Chet," she said mischievously as she hurried them toward the diner. Amanda followed. What in the world was her best friend up to now?

chapter four

Sarah spotted Chet and Milton sitting together in a back booth. The two brothers stood out in the small diner like two sore thumbs, their suits out of place among the denim and plaid worn by the locals. Every patron in the diner was casting glances their way, wondering who the two odd ducks were. Sarah felt sorry for the two brothers and hurried back to their booth. "Mind if we join you for dinner?" she asked politely as she squeezed water out of her hair. The rain had soaked them on the walk over.

Amanda shook rain from the hem of her dress. "I could use a hot tea," she smiled encouragingly at Milton and Chet.

But Chet only studied Amanda warily. The jowls in his face tightened a little, as if he wasn't sure if the two women were being genuinely friendly. But he seemed to make up his mind as he looked at Sarah, and shifted in his seat a little. "Milton, sit by me."

"No, doll face can sit next to me," Milton smiled up at Sarah, obviously pleased. "Maybe romance is in the air after all, huh, sweetheart?"

"Sorry, no," Sarah said apologetically. "Like I said before, only friendship."

Milton sighed melodramatically. "Never hurts to ask twice." He struggled to his feet and slid in next to his brother.

Sarah looked down at the table and spotted the remains of two meatloaf dinners and saw two half-empty cups of coffee. "Amanda," she said and motioned at the booth.

"Why do I always get the window seat," Amanda pretended to complain, smiling prettily at Chet and Milton as she slid down into the vinyl booth.

Sarah sat down next to Amanda. "Well," she smiled, "here we all are."

Anne walked up to the table, plainly curious to know what Amanda and Sarah were doing with the two strangers. She looked at Chet and Milton curiously. "Are you two boys sure you aren't actors?"

"No," Chet replied in a flat voice.

"Doll face," Milton told Anne, "the big screen couldn't handle my handsome mug. Now, how about a refill on the old java, huh?"

Anne shook her head. "What a pair," she said to Sarah and Amanda. "And what will you girls have?"

"I would like a hot lemon tea, a turkey sandwich on rye bread, no crusts, mayonnaise on the side, and a watercress salad with just a splash of nonfat Italian dressing," Amanda said dreamily, without a glance at the menu.

"Well that's too bad, because you're getting a meatloaf plate with mashed potatoes and green beans, a slice of apple pie, and some coffee," Anne informed Amanda. "We don't have all that other nonsense and you know it." She turned to Sarah. "Sarah?"

"The same," Sarah smiled and quickly added. "And make an extra meatloaf plate to go for Andrew, please. He had to stay back at the station but we're headed back there later."

When Sarah said that, she saw Chet glance at Milton. Milton raised his eyebrows and nodded his head as if to agree with his brother that "doll face" was still on duty. "So, you're not here just for a friendly chat, are you, doll face?"

"Well, no," Sarah admitted. "The truth is, I have some questions I hope you guys can answer for me."

"What kind of questions?" Milton asked. Chet waited. He glanced at Amanda and then back at Sarah.

Sarah turned to look at Anne, who was still gawping at the outlandish visitors. "Coffee would be great," she said, tossing a hint into the air.

"Oh, sure," Anne said and finally hurried away.

"What kind of questions," Chet asked Sarah in a monotone, so that it almost didn't sound like a question at all.

"For starters," Sarah said, forcing her voice to sound comfortable and relaxed, "did your father drive to Alaska or fly? I can find the answers to all of my questions with a little old-fashioned detective work, but I'm hoping you two might save me some time."

Milton looked at his brother. Chet sat silently for a moment, slowly turning his coffee cup in his large hands. Sarah had assumed that Milton would take the lead in answering any questions, but to her surprise he seemed to be deferring to his quieter brother. Chet's mind seemed to roam over Sarah's question with patience, as if he were examining every nook and cranny of it. He finally nodded his head at Milton, who replied, "Pop hated to fly. Even when he went to Africa to hunt he always went 'across the pond' on a boat."

"So he drove up to Alaska?" Amanda asked.

"Yes," Chet answered Amanda. He looked at Sarah. "You haven't found Daddy's vehicle?"

"Not yet," Sarah confessed. "Help me out, Mr. Hopski. What type of vehicle would your father have driven in to Alaska?"

"Daddy only hunted in his Subaru."

"You bet," Milton added. "Pop never went on a hunting

trip without his famous Subaru. Or, as we called it, the Green Machine."

"I see," Sarah said in a grateful voice. "And did Mr. Hopski have a hunting cabin around here someplace?"

Both Chet and Milton shrugged their shoulders. "Daddy never told us about his hunting trips. All we know is that he was very particular over his Subaru."

"The only time Pop bragged about a trip was when he bagged a really big game," Milton explained. "Assuming he was in the mood to brag, that is."

Sarah folded her hands together. "Mr. Hopski was found a little ways off an old trail. The trail is called the old Snow Bear Trail, about nine miles north of town. Now, from what I understand about your father, he was a skilled hunter. I don't think he would have been hunting near the old Snow Bear Trail. That's just my opinion, of course. It seems to me that he might have been making his way toward the trail in order to gain a fast path back toward town. I don't believe he was hunting on the Snow Bear Trail. I also don't believe he was lost."

Chet reflected on Sarah's tone and statement. His eyes settled on hers. "You think someone was chasing Daddy?"

"It's possible," Sarah admitted. "Tomorrow morning we're going out to search for your father's hunting cabin. I'm hoping to gather more evidence once we find it. We know that the area around the old Snow Bear Trail is protected, meaning building is not permitted there. That leads me to my working hypothesis: I believe that your father was out hunting when he encountered someone who forced him to run for his life, and he made for the Snow Bear Trail knowing it was a faster route back to town. But he died before he could make it out of the wilderness. This is just my theory, but it's all I have to go on right now."

Chet nodded his head. His eyes glittered a little with that hidden intelligence Sarah had seen before, as he seemed to come to a conclusion. "My brother and me, can we come with you?" he asked.

"You bet," Sarah said with a smile. "As a matter of fact, I was hoping you would ask to come along and—" Sarah stopped talking abruptly. Across the room, the diner door had just swung closed behind Natalie Hopski. And she looked like she was on the warpath.

Natalie quickly spotted Chet and Milton. As she made her way back to the booth, she shook rain off a bright pink umbrella, scattering copious raindrops on the nearby customers who turned to look at this rude stranger. She stomped up to the booth, her oversized galoshes squeaking with every step. She had fury in her eyes. "Why are you talking to them?" she hissed in an ugly tone as she threw a thumb in the direction of Sarah and Amanda. "They are the enemy," she said as if the two women weren't even there.

"Oh, cool your crows' feet," Milton said and waved his hand at Natalie. "We're just chatting."

"Cops don't just 'chat,' you moron," Natalie snapped at Milton.

Milton's cheeks grew red. "Back off, Natalie," he said in a voice that betrayed the depths of his anger. "You ain't my boss. Never have been, never will be. You can't just show up and boss me around like you did when we were kids, got it? I'm a grown man and I can speak to whoever I choose." He heaved a breath when he finished, his cheeks slightly red as if holding his tongue.

"You're a pathetic little runt who—"

"Enough," Sarah told Natalie in a firm voice and stood up. "Ms. Hopski, if you can't speak in a cordial tone then I'm going to have to ask you to leave. You're disturbing the other patrons and I will not tolerate that."

Natalie stared into Sarah's eyes. "Make me leave," she dared Sarah.

Sarah drew in a deep breath. Natalie was fishing for a

reason to sue the police department for harassment most likely, in the hopes of tying up their hands. "Please, don't start something you don't want to finish."

"Oh, please," Natalie said insultingly. "It's time for you to learn your place, girly."

But before Sarah could reply, Amanda slid out of the booth and threw her finger in Natalie's face. "You and me, outside, you disgusting bully!" she said in a fierce tone. "I'm going to mop the sidewalk with that rat's nest you call a hairdo."

"How dare you," Natalie said and wound her arm back to slap Amanda. Chet caught her wrist.

"Leave," he told Natalie in a voice that sent a chill through Sarah, who could also see his surprising strength as he restrained Natalie's substantial arm. Chet barely moved in his seat, but Natalie twisted in his grasp as if in pain.

Natalie finally pulled away from Chet and slowly began backing away. "We're not finished," she promised Sarah and Amanda, her galoshes squeaking on the floor. "No one speaks to Natalie Hopski this way and gets away with it. My lawyer is going to eat you two alive!"

"Out!" Chet said in a low rumble and pointed at the front door. Natalie flinched and hurried back outside into the rain. Quiet settled over the diner once again and the other customers turned back to their meals, trying not to gossip too loudly about what they had just witnessed.

"What a snake," Milton said, shaking his head.

"She ain't our sister," Chet told Milton as he turned back to his coffee, as if nothing had happened.

Milton turned to Amanda. "Hey, you're not half bad."

"For an English woman," Chet added quietly. Sarah smiled a little as she realized this giant of a man was actually teasing Amanda.

"Don't mess with my tea and scones," Amanda teased

back. She sat down and shook her head. "How can you two put up with that woman?"

Sarah sat back down, grateful that Chet had intervened before the confrontation could go any further. "Natalie sure did listen to you," she commented to Chet.

"That's because Chet stopped being her door mat years ago," Milton said in a proud voice and patted Chet on the shoulder. "My brother gave me the courage to stand up to that jelly roll bully, too."

Amanda tried not to laugh but she couldn't help it. "Sorry," she said, bursting into laughter. "Oh my...jelly roll bully...oh dear."

Sarah saw Chet grin sheepishly. "Hey, if the shoe fits," Milton grinned, "wear it."

Sarah glanced around and saw faces staring at the raucous laughter coming from their booth. She cleared her throat. "Amanda, dear, try to control yourself."

"Jelly roll bully," Amanda cried in a desperate whisper and slapped the table.

Sarah sighed. What was the use in trying? "Chet, there are more questions I would like to ask you, but not here. It's obvious my partner is having difficulties focusing."

Chet grinned a little bit wider. "It's good to see people laugh. In my family laughter was scarce even on a good day."

"You got that right, brother," Milton dove in. "In our house, Pop and Ma sure had their bouts, but it was mostly Natalie causing the trouble. By the time she was a teenager we were all ducking for cover. Her and Ma especially went at it like two wet cats in a burlap sack."

Chet shook his head, disapproving. "I heard Momma tell Daddy once that Natalie was evil."

Amanda stopped laughing. Chet's tone quickly sobered her mind. "Oh, Chet. You don't think your mother really thought that, do you?"

Chet looked down at his large hands encircling his coffee

mug and then looked back up at Amanda. "Momma didn't think I could understand her. She used to rant and rave to Daddy when I was in the room, like I was invisible. I know what people think about me, ma'am. They look at me and they see a giant, an oaf, an idiot. A circus freak."

"You're not a circus freak," Amanda promised Chet. She reached across the table and patted his hand. "I'm sorry you went through such things as a child. I just met you, but I can tell you have a very gentle heart. And you may not speak often, but when you do, you're clearly a very intelligent man. No one should judge a book by its cover."

Chet blushed. Amanda's sincerity touched his heart. He looked at Sarah, determined to go on. "Daddy said that too – never judge a book by its cover. Daddy never liked the rich people he sold homes to. Daddy always liked the underdog." Chet looked down at his hand again. "Daddy gave us a good life. Momma and Daddy loved us so much. Natalie never appreciated it."

"Natalie hated Pop," Milton said in a matter-of-fact voice. "Natalie hated Ma, too. And to this day I believe Natalie pushed Ma down the stairs."

"Stairs?" Sarah asked, a little shocked. Peter's background check certainly hadn't turned up this tidbit.

Milton made a sour face. "Oh yes, hot stuff. Pop loved Ma. Oh, boy, did he. Those two were inseparable...real love, you know? When we were teenagers – Natalie was about sixteen – Pop took us all on vacation to Europe—"

"London," Chet said and looked at Amanda.

"Yeah, London first," Milton continued. "Anyways, the first day we got there, Natalie had a huge fight with Pop and Ma, demanding a bigger allowance, a separate room, all kinds of other stuff. She loved to play Pop and Ma off each other, and in the end, just to get some peace and quiet probably, Pop told Ma to take Natalie shopping. Maybe if he hadn't..." Milton shook his head in disgust. "Long story short, Ma fell down a flight of stairs in the fancy store where they were shopping. It was near the winter holiday and the store was jammed full of shoppers, so there were lots of witnesses, but you better bet that most of them scattered when it happened. One store clerk later swore she saw Natalie push her, but another clerk swore a statement that Natalie had been in a dressing room the whole time. The department store owner was desperate to get it cleared up and covered up so there was just a quick investigation, an 'Inquest' they called it, in front of a judge. Ma's death was ruled accidental. Pop continued to baby our beloved sister even though she continued to torture him. He could not bring himself to believe she killed the only woman he ever loved." Milton sighed and ran a tired hand over his eyes.

"How awful," Amanda said and nearly began crying.

Sarah leaned back in the booth and folded her arms. She looked into the eyes of the Hopski brothers and saw real pain – the type of pain that damages the heart for life – rise up like a ghost. "Excuse me," Chet said, "I need to...use the bathroom."

Milton stood up to let Chet out of the booth. Chet lumbered away, wiping at his eyes. "Big guy never got over Ma's death," Milton told Sarah and Amanda quietly. "He loved Ma more than life, even if Ma underestimated him. Ma loved him fiercely. She loved me, too. She was one special lady," Milton said. Without a word, he walked off after Chet with watery eyes.

Sarah felt her heart break. "Amanda—"

"Don't say a word because I know exactly what you're thinking, Los Angeles. Natalie Hopski is going down, and so is that little scarecrow Charlene," Amanda promised, wiping the corner of her eye with a napkin.

"Within the law," Sarah cautioned. She felt anger grip her heart. "I feel so bad for those two guys."

"Me, too," Amanda replied. "I mean, here they are, set for

life with more money than we'll ever see, and yet...they're a little bit broken inside. Or maybe more than a little bit. It's so sad."

"We need to see Mr. Hopski's will," Sarah said resolutely. "From this point forward, we're going to conduct an intense investigation, turn over every stone, investigate every possibility, and step on two vicious spiders."

"I'm with you, all the way," Amanda promised. "Los Angeles, I think I'm beginning to understand why being a cop is so important. I know cops get a bad name, but I also know there are some really good cops in this world like yourself." Amanda patted Sarah's arm. "I'm proud to have you as my best friend, love. We've been through the ringer together and I'm not backing down now."

"I know, June Bug," Sarah replied in a grateful voice. "I didn't think that you would back down, not after seeing the faces of those two poor men after that story."

"That's right, sister," Amanda stated in a fighting voice. "My armor is on and I'm ready to hit the battlefield. So tell me, what's our first move?"

"We still have to search for Mr. Hopski's hunting cabin and Subaru."

"You mean we can't do anything tonight?"

"We can't get the will faxed up from his lawyer until tomorrow, June Bug," Sarah explained.

"Drat."

"Well," Sarah said and rubbed her chin, "maybe there is something we can do."

"What?"

"Invite Chet and Milton out to my cabin," Sarah said, her voice quickening as she thought it through. "It'll be safer to talk there. I have a lot of questions and I want Chet and Milton as comfortable as possible. I need to nudge at them, but with gentle gloves. Not to mention, they might be safer at my cabin than at the lodge. Just in case."

"Got it," Amanda stated and looked over her shoulder. She saw Anne approaching with two meatloaf plates in her hands. Suddenly, she wasn't hungry anymore.

Chet liked Sarah's cabin and immediately settled onto the couch to read his evening Bible verses. Milton, on the other hand, roamed around the kitchen for a few minutes, then pronounced the cabin a little cramped. "No offense, hot stuff," he said, finally sitting down on the living room couch and folding his arms together, "it's just a little tight for my taste. I'm used to big, open beach houses, right on the ocean." He cracked his knuckles, looking around a little nervously.

Sarah grinned. Milton reminded her of a washed-up 1950s mafia boss running quarters at a run-down laundromat. "I'm sorry my cabin doesn't live up to your standards."

"Oh, no worries," Milton promised, trying to stretch his short legs. "You like a little cabin, I like a big beach pad. Hey, we all have different taste, hot stuff."

Chet looked up from his Bible. "I like your cabin, ma'am."

"Please, call me Sarah."

Chet nodded as if he wasn't quite sure about becoming so friendly. Even though he liked Sarah, he was still uncertain if he wanted to become friends with her. "Okay," he said, turning back to the book in his lap.

"Coffee," Amanda announced, bursting into the living room carrying an antique wooden tray with four mugs full of steaming hot coffee. She set the tray on the polished coffee table in front of the couch and sat down in the wingback armchair next to the fireplace. "There are cinnamon rolls warming in the oven."

"Hey, Chet loves cinnamon rolls," Milton said and nudged Chet on the arm. "Isn't that right?"

"Yes," Chet said and blushed a little. "Daddy and me always loved cinnamon rolls."

Sarah sat down in an armchair next to the couch and relaxed. Night had fallen and the soft rain had turned harder, soaking the darkness outside with mystery. "Guys, I want to ask you a very deep and personal question, okay? But please, if you don't feel like answering, then don't. You're here voluntarily. I would never force you to answer any question that would make you feel uncomfortable."

"You want to know if we think Natalie and Charlene are behind Pop's death, right, hot stuff?"

"I'm inclined to believe you have both already hinted at that, but I would like to touch deeper on the subject, if that's alright with the both of you," Sarah replied.

"Chet?" Milton asked.

Chet closed the book in his lap carefully. He looked over to the fireplace and contemplated the dry logs waiting to be lit on a cold, wintry night. "Okay."

Milton nodded his head. "Okay, doll face, ask away."

"Actually, before we begin with Natalie and Charlene, I would like to ask about your father's will," Sarah explained. "All four of you traveled to Alaska even though the body – your father – could have been easily delivered to you by air freight. My guess is," Sarah drew in a calm breath, "Natalie and Charlene want to make sure the autopsy report determines that the death was accidental. You two, on the other hand—"

"Know it wasn't," Milton cut in. "Chet and I know Natalie and Charlene killed Pop...somehow. We're not sure yet, but we intend to find out how. And boy, aren't you a diamond in the rough up here, doll face. Does Snow Falls know what a gem they've got in you? Your reputation back home ranks up there with the big boys. You took down some pretty serious killers in your time."

"Natalie wasn't happy when she found out you live here," Chet added. "Neither was Charlene."

Sarah sat silent for a few seconds while her mind stored away Chet's words. Somehow, she had not anticipated that they would have gone as far as looking up the various law enforcement personnel in town. "I see," she finally said. "That's why she burst into the diner. She wanted to interrupt our meeting."

"Natalie warned us to stay away from you," Chet admitted.

Milton patted Chet on his arm. "And you sure told her where to stick it," he said in a proud voice.

Amanda's cheeks turned pink as if she had bitten her tongue. "Uh...excuse me," she said and ran out of the living room.

Milton tossed a thumb toward the kitchen. "Your friend liked my joke, huh?"

Sarah sighed. "I'm sure she's just fetching the cinnamon rolls, don't mind her."

"Not at all," Chet said mildly.

"Okay, we are agreed that Natalie and Charlene are possibly responsible—"

"Not possibly," Milton cut in. "Those two are demons sent straight from—"

"Language," Chet warned Milton.

Milton bit his tongue. "Sure, yeah, sorry," he said. "Natalie and Charlene killed Pop."

"Okay," Sarah continued. "If we agree on that, then how could they have done it?"

"Natalie is evil," Milton insisted. "She knows too many people. She's got her fingers in too many pies. She even pressured the mayor of Los Angeles to get the fuzz to begin hunting for Pop."

"When was this?" Sarah asked. She remembered Pete's mention of this and was intrigued to hear more.

"Let's see...Pop left for Alaska...I mean, he vanished on us shortly before the holiday shopping season. About two weeks later, Natalie started fussing at the mayor," Milton explained. "Usually they wouldn't file a missing person report because there was no evidence of distress, but she greased some palms to make it happen."

Sarah quickly mapped a time frame in her mind. "Any idea if Natalie or Charlene might have hired someone to carry out their plan? Some friend of theirs, perhaps?" she asked, her patient voice hiding her mounting frustration.

Chet slowly folded his arms together. "Natalie never had a friend."

Milton nodded in agreement. "She's too calculating for that. But money can buy people, so who knows who Natalie might have bought?"

"Do you believe your sister would have hired a professional killer to go after Mr. Hopski?" Sarah asked.

Chet shook his head no adamantly. "Natalie doesn't like strangers."

"What Chet means to say is that she's the type that likes to do the dirty work herself...like when she killed Ma," Milton chimed in. He leaned forward and snatched up a mug of coffee and handed it to Chet. "Natalie wouldn't have found a gun for hire to go after Pop, no way."

Sarah watched Milton take a mug of coffee for himself and add four packets of sugar, then sit back and take a grateful gulp. "What about Charlene? Perhaps Natalie instructed her to hire—"

"No way, doll face, you're barking up the wrong tree," Milton told Sarah as he shook his head. "No way Natalie would let Charlene have that kind of advantage on her. No way in the world. Natalie is playing Charlene like a fiddle because she thinks it'll get her to her goal, but she would never give Charlene a chance to take the reins like that."

Milton's statement made sense to Sarah. "Where were

Natalie and Charlene during the two weeks Mr. Hopski vanished?"

"You mean before Natalie started nagging at the mayor?" Milton asked.

"Yes."

Milton shrugged his shoulders. "Who knows? Like I said, doll face, when Pop went on a hunting trip, he would just up and leave without saying a word. I didn't even know Pop was missing until Natalie called me and told me to meet her at the mayor's office."

Sarah mused on this, taking in the information Milton was pouring out. "How about you, Chet?" she asked.

"Teresa and I were on a cruise," Chet explained. "Teresa likes to take cruises to the Bahamas." Chet gave Sarah a grave look. "Natalie waited until I was gone," he said and she saw his right hand ball into a fist on the arm of the couch.

"Yep," Milton said in a disgusted voice, "that bat waited until the muscle was out of town, that's for sure."

Sarah stared into Chet's eyes. The man was speaking the truth. "Guys, where did your father keep his hunting Subaru?"

"In his garage," Milton stated.

"And you checked to make sure his Subaru was missing, right?"

Chet nodded his head. "I checked when we got back from the cruise."

"Did you check his bedroom?"

"For what, doll face?" Milton asked.

"Oh, clothes missing, toothbrush and deodorant gone. You know, items that would indicate he had packed for a trip," Sarah explained.

"Well," Milton said and sipped on his coffee, "I took a look in Pop's room. Everything seemed okay." Milton lowered the coffee mug from his face. "But Pop lives in a mansion, hot stuff. It takes me days to get from the front door to the kitchen. And don't get me started on the size of Pop's bedroom. Oh boy."

"Daddy has a really big master suite with a private bathroom," Chet explained. "Charlene said it didn't matter if he was missing, I still shouldn't go in there. He was real private about his room. But I did see his toothbrush and deodorant in the bathroom."

"Hey, wait a minute," Milton interrupted. "And I saw the cup he soaked his false teeth in. Would he have left without that?"

Chet sipped on his coffee. "Also, Daddy's closet had a little row of empty clothes hangers and his green camouflage duffel bag was gone."

"Good eye," Sarah complimented Chet, who blushed a little.

"It's hard to know for sure, but it seems like someone got messy and left behind some crumbs," Sarah told Chet. She leaned forward and picked up a coffee mug. As she did, Amanda reappeared, carrying a platter heaped with hot, fresh cinnamon buns. She handed everyone a plate and then sat down next to Milton. "Better?" Sarah asked.

Amanda nodded her head. "Better," she promised.

Chet took a bite of his cinnamon bun. "Good," he said.

Milton followed after Chet. "Hey, not bad," he complimented Amanda. "Your husband is a lucky guy to have a great chef like you in the kitchen."

"Well, my husband is currently driving me crazy with a certain bell," Amanda explained, as she retrieved the last mug of coffee. "My husband has a broken leg because he refused to listen to his wife when she begged him not to go up onto the roof of our cabin and knock snow off."

"Ouch," Milton said and continued to work on his cinnamon roll.

Chet nodded his head slowly. "I broke my leg when I was seventeen years old. It hurt."

"I bet it did, love." Amanda couldn't help but smile. Chet had such a flat demeanor, but she was beginning to understand that he was very sympathetic.

Sarah took a bite of her cinnamon roll and listened to the rain fall outside. In her mind's eye, she wondered if Natalie and Charlene were lurking somewhere outside in the shadows. "Excuse me, please," she said and stood up. "I need to make a quick call."

Sarah put down her coffee and plate and hurried into the kitchen, grabbed the phone, and called the lodge where Natalie and Charlene were staying. "Yes, this is Sarah Garland. I'm acting detective while Detective Spencer is away."

A very bored young lady yawned into the phone as if she had just moments ago put down her Nancy Drew novel. "Sure, I know who you are. Everyone in town knows who you are."

"Oh," Sarah said, wondering if that was a compliment or insult. "I need to know if two of your guests are currently at the lodge."

"You mean the big lady and the skinny lady from California?"

"Uh, yes," Sarah said and fought back a grin. The young lady pronounced 'California' like it was in a foreign language.

"Nope. They left about an hour ago, about ten minutes apart. And good riddance. My parents have owned this lodge since I was born and we have never had any trouble with a guest until today," the young lady complained.

"I'm sorry."

"So am I," the young lady said gloomily. "Anything else I can do for you?"

"No, that's it. Thank you." Sarah hung up the phone and looked around the kitchen. "An hour ago," she whispered. "Now, where did those two get off to?" she wondered.

Amanda walked into the kitchen. "What's going on, Los Angeles? You looked worried."

"Natalie Hopski and Charlene Nelton left the lodge about an hour ago, according to the front desk clerk."

"You mean Shelly Brights?" Amanda said. "I know her. The only girl in town who doesn't know that smiling is a good thing. And what a shame, too. Shelly is a pretty girl, but her depressed attitude makes people run the other way."

"She didn't sound very happy when I spoke to her, either," Sarah agreed and walked over to the back door, looking out at the rain. She checked that the deadbolt was secure. "I'm sure Natalie Hopski and Charlene Nelton doesn't know where I live, so they can't be headed here. But that leaves me to wonder where those two went off to?"

"Maybe they went to meet the killer?"

Sarah went back to the phone and called Andrew. "Natalie Hopski and Charlene Nelton left the lodge. Do you have a man following them?"

Andrew sounded distracted. "Uh...no," he apologized. "Old Man Trapp swerved to hit a deer out on Ice Ridge Road and slammed his truck into a power pole. His truck caught fire." Sarah could hear Andrew scratching his leg even through the phone. "I'm sorry...I'm dealing with a vehicle fire and a power outage, Sarah. I had to send my guys out to the scene of the accident."

"When did this happen?" Sarah asked.

"I called the patrol away from the lodge about an hour ago," Andrew told Sarah.

"Okay, Andrew, I understand. You did the right thing. Is Mr. Trapp okay?"

"He's bruised a little but none the worse for wear, I guess," Andrew replied. "The roads are slippery with the rain and it's dark. I can't really jump down the poor man's throat."

"No, you can't," Sarah answered, but she wasn't thinking of Mr. Trapp.

"Say, is everything okay?" Andrew asked Sarah in a worried voice.

"Natalie Hopski and Charlene Nelton left the lodge about an hour ago," Sarah explained. "About the same time you pulled the patrol away to go handle Mr. Trapp's accident."

"That's not good, is it?" Andrew asked.

"Not really. But you can't arrest two people for leaving the lodge, either." Sarah bit down on her lip. "Chet and Milton Hopski are still at my cabin with me and Amanda. We're having a question and answer session. I'll fill you in on the details tomorrow morning."

"Do I still need to pick you up at Amanda's cabin in the morning?"

"We'll meet you at the police station instead," Sarah told Andrew and hung up. "Well," she told Amanda, "two snakes are loose in the rain and we don't know where they're at." Sarah looked toward the living room. "Our best option is to continue asking questions while we can."

Amanda looked at the back door. She listened to the rain falling outside. "And hope no one else shows up."

"Exactly," replied Sarah grimly. She headed back into the living room with a false smile on to hide the bad feeling that had settled in her gut like a brick.

chapter five

Sarah glanced up at a low, overcast sky. The rain had stopped, leaving behind a gloomy, miserable dampness that chilled her to the bone. "Rain, rain, go away," she whispered and kicked at a rock with one rain boot. The Snow Bear Trail was soaked from the rain and the lush spring landscape showed no signs of drying up anytime soon. Rain boots and a dark gray rain jacket protected her from the damp but caused a heavy feeling to soak her heart. "Is this the place?" she asked Andrew as she surveyed the landscape. Andrew had driven her the several miles up the trail to the place closest to where the body had been found.

Andrew leaned back against his green truck and pointed off into the distance. Bright yellow police tape was tied to four large, powerful trees, forming a solid square perimeter around where Mr. Hopski's body had been found. "That's the place."

Amanda stood next to Sarah and shivered. She shoved her hands down into the pockets of her bright pink rain coat and looked around. "We're really far out," she said in a worried voice. "You never really realize how big Alaska is until you're out here. It's like a person could just vanish and never be seen again...like the land could just swallow a person whole."

"Yep," Andrew agreed and yawned. He was wearing a bright orange vest over a brown wool shirt and a pair of blue jeans instead of his uniform. His face was sleepy and his hair was messy. Evidently the emergency with Mr. Trapp's truck and the power lines had taken most of the night to clear away and Andrew had barely dragged himself out of bed to meet them at the police station that morning. "I'm not sure what we're going to find out here, Sarah."

Sarah looked around. Anyone could be watching her. And even though she had her gun and Andrew was holding his rifle, she still felt unsafe. "We won't know until we look," she said and began walking toward the taped-off area. Andrew looked at Amanda and nodded toward Sarah. Amanda nodded back and hurried to follow her best friend. Andrew took a quick look around and got moving.

Sarah walked through knee-high grass and stopped when she came to the edge of a thick line of trees. Beyond the woods, she heard the sound of a river flowing and immediately thought of Peter. Surely the river was full of delicious trout that would excite her old partner to no end. "Maybe someday, Pete," she whispered and looked over her shoulder at Amanda. "Are you okay, June Bug?"

"Sleepy, cranky, damp and a bit chilly, but okay," Amanda told Sarah with a grin. "I wish we hadn't stayed up so late last night asking a million and one questions." Amanda yawned. "I think I got three hours of sleep after I drove home."

"Too much bell?" Sarah asked.

Amanda nodded her head. "That bloody bell."

"Sorry," Sarah winced.

Amanda shrugged her shoulders. "Love is grand in the spring...except when a bloody bell is involved."

Sarah patted Amanda on her shoulder. "Hang tough," she said and focused on the police tape. "Andrew, where exactly was the body...I mean, Mr. Hopski found?"

Andrew walked up to Sarah, studied the overcast sky, and then pointed at a large tree. "Over there near that tree," he said and lifted the police tape. "Ladies first."

Sarah and Amanda ducked under the yellow crime scene tape and walked over to the tree. Sarah flipped on the detective switch in her mind and focused only on the scene before her eyes. She methodically examined the area where Mr. Hopski's body was found, and the positions of his belongings, which had been bagged up as evidence but were still signaled with numbered markers on the ground. "Andrew, which way was Mr. Hopski's head facing when you found him?"

Andrew rubbed at his eyes a little, thinking back. "Let's see," he said and knelt down, "when I arrived, the old man was laying this way," he said and sketched an outline on the wet ground with his right finger, "so his head would have been facing...east...toward the trail."

Sarah looked toward the trail. "So, assuming he wasn't moved, if he fell like that then Mr. Hopski was walking toward the trail and not away from it."

Andrew stood up. "Yeah, that makes sense," he said, squinting as if forcing his mind to wake up.

Amanda watched Sarah make small loops around the taped off area. "If Mr. Hopski was facing east, he was traveling from the west," she said, then stopped pacing and looked into the thick wilderness. "Andrew, I have a compass in my pocket. I want to walk a few miles west, okay?"

Andrew nodded his head. "I thought as much," he said. "Stay here." Andrew jogged back to his truck and returned with two cans of bright orange spray paint. "Here," he said and handed Sarah a can of the spray paint, "we'll mark our path."

"Good thinking," Sarah told Andrew as he shook the can of spray paint to mix it. "June Bug, are you up for a hike?"

"Sure, why not," Amanda forced a smile to her face.

Sarah grew silent and listened to the sound of the river in the silence of the deep woods. Andrew caught notice of her face. "That's the Trout River that runs out toward the coast," he explained.

"Oh, I know what river it is," Sarah told Andrew in a polite tone, "I was just wondering if Mr. Hopski used the river as a road? I'm wondering if he was familiar with this area, if he ever hunted here before." Sarah shook her head. "No sense in wondering over questions I can't answer right now. Andrew, lead the way."

Andrew hesitated. "Listen, ladies, there's a lot of mean bears roaming around in these woods. My rifle can rip a bear in half, but that's not to say we can walk around like we're on a picnic," he said in a stern tone. "Sarah, take your gun out and keep it at the ready. Amanda, stay between me and Sarah at all times. I'll lead and Sarah will cover the rear. If you see or hear anything let me know. I'm a good shot, but I don't have eyes in the back of my head."

"You think...we might run into a bear?" Amanda asked worriedly.

Andrew couldn't say. "Maybe. There's always a chance. Grizzly bears live mostly up in the high country, but we could run into a black bear. Don't really matter what kind of bear we might run into, either. All bears are dangerous. Got it?"

"Got it," Amanda promised.

"Got it," Sarah assured Andrew, grateful that Andrew was a skilled outdoorsman. Sure, maybe the guy wasn't the smoothest cop in the world, but he was an Alaskan man through and through, and he knew his stuff when it came to the wild.

Andrew hesitated again. He looked into the woods. "Sarah, one more thing. If you don't live in Alaska and you come up here hunting bears, you're required to have a licensed guide with you in the field. And you must stop and pick up some big game locking-tags. Now, if you're hunting a black bear, a guide isn't required. I made a few calls last night and talked to a friend at the Alaska Department of Fish and Game and had him run some checks on Mr. Hopski. We came up empty-handed. Mr. Hopski had never registered a kill on a bear in Alaska, picked up any locking-tags, nothing. So if he was up here hunting bears like his kids said, it could only have been for black bears."

"And you're just telling us this now?" Amanda fussed.

Andrew shrugged his shoulders. "I was going to show you the report when we got back to my office," Andrew explained. "I've had four hours sleep, ladies. Sorry if my mind isn't catching up to my mouth yet."

"No, sorry I fussed," Amanda apologized. "I guess we're all a bit cranky." Amanda looked at Sarah. Only Sarah seemed fully awake. "What are you thinking Los Angeles?"

Sarah stared off into the woods. "Could be Mr. Hopski hunted illegally," she suggested. "Money does buy people hidden, undeserved privileges. Or it could be the man never came here to hunt to begin with."

"What do you mean?" Andrew asked.

"Maybe Mr. Hopski came to Alaska to rest," Sarah suggested. "From what I understand, he liked hunting in Africa. And anyway, why would a man his age come to Alaska during the winter months? It's not just cold, but the bears would be in hibernation. It doesn't make sense."

"I was wondering that myself," Andrew told Sarah. "But Mr. Hopski was an old man, and from what I understand, he was kinda eccentric, too. I figured he might have been new to the game of hunting bear and didn't understand the proper season to hunt in. I hate jumping to conclusions, you know, so I didn't say anything initially. It ain't my place to judge a man."

"But it is your place to ask logical questions," Sarah reminded Andrew. "You're a cop, and it's your duty to kick over every stone."

Andrew kicked at the ground. "I know that Sarah, but I've never been the pushy type. Nagging away at people is hard for me. I know I'm a cop, but sometimes my politeness gets in the way."

Sarah wasn't in the mood to coddle a cop who was licking his wounds. "Time to stop being polite," she said in a professional tone. "Today we're cops and nothing else. All of us," Sarah said and pointed at Amanda for emphasis. "A man was murdered and we're out to find out why and who did it. Is everybody on board?"

"You bet," Andrew said and checked his rifle.

"Yes, love, I'm on board," Amanda promised. "Andrew, lead the way."

Andrew nodded his head and stepped into the woods. Amanda followed. Sarah took up the rear. "We'll move slow," Andrew called back over his shoulder. He walked a few yards, stopped, and marked a large tree trunk with the spray paint.

Sarah kept her eyes peeled, searching every tree, every fallen log, every sound, with patient skill. Thirty minutes later, she was completely engulfed in the woods, miles from the groomed trail, not to mention miles away from any road, house, building or human being other than Amanda and Andrew. The depth of the woods sent a solemn, lonely feeling into Sarah's heart that no words could explain. Instead of speaking, she looked at the river that surged out of a gap in the trees next to where they stood. The river was filled with wild rapids, racing over and past large rocks on an urgent mission that no man could understand. The river was untamed, free, and deadly. "Beautiful," Sarah said, standing on a low cliff and staring down at the river.

"The river is wild out here," Andrew agreed, "but calmer more toward town. I wouldn't recommend going for a swim in those waters."

Amanda stared down at the raging waters. The chilling

image of people attempting to raft down this wild river came into her mind. She saw a group of people wearing red and blue helmets and life vests tossed headlong into the river and carried into a watery abyss under the churning surface. A shiver walked down her spine. As much as she loved Alaska, the dangerous rapids scared her. That's when she wondered if dangerous rapids scared Mr. Hopski, too.

"Hey," Amanda said, signaling the other two to stop. "I just noticed there's no place to cross over to the other side. Mr. Hopski would had to have been on this side of the river unless he was the world's greatest swimmer. Even if he was, I doubt he would chance a swim in freezing waters at his age."

Sarah smiled. "You're getting it, girl," she said. "We'll stay on this side of the river and keep moving."

Andrew checked his rifle again and looked around. So far, there had been no sign of bears, not even a footprint. "I guess we're good for now," he said and checked his watch. "Okay, let's move."

Sarah marked a tree with her spray paint and got moving. She followed Andrew and Amanda deeper into the woods and didn't stop walking until an hour passed, almost without her noticing it. "Hey," Andrew said and waved his hands at Sarah and Amanda, "look at this."

Sarah felt a jolt of electricity shoot through her heart. She raced up to Andrew with Amanda at her side. Andrew bent down and examined two pieces of cut rope that lay on the trail. From their size, they looked perfect for tying a person's hands and feet together. "Now why would this rope be way out here?"

Sarah moved next to Andrew, studying it as close as she dared. And there, like a sweet blessing, she spotted a single arm hair caught in the rope. "Hello, there," she whispered and pulled a plastic evidence bag from her right pocket. Andrew passed her a latex glove from his pocket so she could gingerly place the ropes inside the bag. "Andrew, you're a great cop. Never think otherwise," she said.

Andrew smiled from ear to ear. "Thanks."

"So, does this mean we turn back?" Amanda asked in a hopeful voice.

"Nope," Sarah said and pointed forward. "We need to keep walking and—" Sarah stopped talking when she heard the sound of a large creature thrashing through the woods. "Uh, Andrew—"

Andrew dropped down onto one knee and aimed his rifle into the woods and fired off a few warning shots. Just barely in the distance they could glimpse a massive, dark shape half-hidden in the tangle of bushes as it raced toward them. At the sound of the shots, the bear suddenly changed direction and lumbered quickly away. "Okay," Amanda said shakily when the noise had faded, "that's enough for me today. I'm walking back to the truck."

"Come on, June Bug," Sarah told Amanda and took her hand, "we can't stop now. Besides, we have Andrew."

Andrew stood up and brushed off his knee with his left hand. "Don't let that bear scare you," he said and pointed forward. "It will think twice before coming back. Come on."

Amanda looked into Sarah's eyes. Sarah smiled. "Oh, alright," she caved in. "I guess we can't stop now."

"That's my girl," Sarah said and they walked deeper and deeper into the woods. Another hour passed without turning up anything of interest. Sarah was about to suggest they turn back when out of nowhere, a trail appeared, cutting away from the river. "Andrew?"

Andrew shook his head. "I've never seen this trail in my life. I've also never hunted this area before, either. I hunt more south." Andrew studied the trail. "But I studied the map pretty closely, and this isn't anywhere on it. But the trail is old...looks like it's been here a while. I guess we need to follow it."

"Oh joy," Amanda groaned. She watched Andrew mark a tree with his spray paint. "I don't know what's worse, this trail or that bear who's probably waiting for us!"

"Come on," Sarah urged Amanda and followed Andrew down the trail and away from the river. Twenty minutes later the trail ended at an old, run-down cabin next to a muddy field just large enough for a small plane to land in. The cabin appeared deserted and dangerous—at least, that's how Sarah saw the matter, eyeing the battered shutters, the small porch missing many floorboards, and the general disrepair. But the cabin was simply a utilitarian place for the kind of travelers who didn't need many creature comforts. "I think we found Mr. Hopski's hunting cabin," she said in a hushed, relieved voice and patted Amanda on her shoulder. "Come on partner, let's have a look inside."

Amanda wasn't so sure she wanted to walk into a creepy cabin in the middle of the wilderness. But she also didn't want to be left standing alone outside. "Maybe there's coffee inside," she said skittishly, and followed Sarah and Andrew inside.

The inside of the cabin was cold, dark and dusty. When they forced open the creaky front door, they found a single large room with a stone fireplace, an old wood-burning stove, a sink, a sleeping cot, and a few other sticks of furniture gathering dust in the darkness. Andrew searched the gloom and then spotted a kerosene lantern sitting on the wooden table. He quickly eased over the creaking floorboards to light the lantern with a pack of matches he had brought along. The lantern threw out enough light to give life to the room. "Almost full," Andrew said as he shook the kerosene lantern a little. He set it back down on the wooden table. "Wick isn't burned down that much, either."

Sarah closed the front door and looked around. A wooden bookshelf was pushed up against the east wall. She walked over the bookshelf and examined books covered with dust. "Classics," she said, and took one off the shelf. "Classics that are worth a lot of money, too," she commented, fingering the expensive binding and noticing the early printing dates. Sarah put down the book and focused on the room. As her eyes adjusted to the lantern's glow she could see a few richly detailed paintings on the wall that seemed out of place for a hunting cabin. "Mr. Hopski was found with a wallet full of money...and now it looks like his cabin is untouched...I do think someone wanted his death to appear accidental," she half-whispered to Amanda and Andrew.

Amanda folded her arms together and decided to check for coffee in the cabinets mounted over the rusty white sink. She reached up and tugged one of the cabinet doors. As soon as she did, a bag of sugar dropped out. Amanda screamed, thinking the bag of sugar was a rat. Andrew jumped and started to run toward Amanda. As he did, his right foot dropped down through a rotted piece of floorboard and got stuck. "Darn floor," he cursed and began trying to pull his foot free.

Amanda grabbed her heart and bent down to retrieve the sugar. "Darn bag of sugar," she exclaimed, set it back in the cupboard, and walked over to Andrew. "Here, give me your hand."

Andrew placed his rifle down onto the floor and grabbed Amanda's hand. Amanda braced herself and gave one hard yank. Andrew's foot came flying out of the hole, and along with it, a small section of rotted floorboards fell away. He stepped back and waved away the dust that erupted into the air, peering down at the floor. "Hey, look at that," he said and bent over. From the space beneath the floorboards he picked up a book and brushed the dust off its red leather cover. "It looks like some kind of a journal."

Sarah walked over to Andrew and took the book from him. "It is a journal," she said and looked at Andrew with grateful eyes. "You're two for two today."

"Well, it's really nothing," Andrew said in a humble voice. "I was only doing my job."

Sarah smiled, walked over to the wooden table, pulled back a nice wooden chair, and sat down. "Let's see what's inside," she said as she opened the front cover and began reading. "Guys, this is the journal of one William Archie Hopski," she announced.

Andrew snatched up his rifle off the floor and hurried over to Sarah. Amanda followed. "Well, I'll be," he said.

"Listen to this," Sarah said and began reading the first journal entry. "My beloved wife has been taken away from me. My heart has now been torn beyond repair. I have decided to return back to our cabin and rest in my memories of her for a while, leaving my children to believe I have once again traveled to Africa on one of my many make-believe hunting trips. I have given my children everything, but this cabin belongs only to me and my beloved wife. Perhaps someday we will be together again. The pain is too much to bear to continue writing. That's the end of the entry." Sarah closed the journal. A single tear slipped from her eye. "Very sad," she whispered.

Amanda wiped a tear from her eye. "That poor, poor, dear man."

Andrew cleared his throat and fought back a tear. "Yeah, well, maybe we should be getting back, huh? Walking out always takes longer than walking in."

Sarah nodded her head and stood up. "Let's take a good look around first, Andrew. You look inside the wood stove. Amanda check the cabinets. I'll check the bookshelf again and look behind the paintings and then we'll check that small airfield out back and see if there are any fresh tracks." Andrew and Amanda agreed and got to work.

"Wood has barely been burned," Andrew announced, studying the contents inside the wood stove.

"Cabinets are full of provisions...dishes are clean...sink is dry," Amanda called out to Sarah.

Sarah checked the books on the bookshelf and then looked behind every painting. She came up empty-handed. Next, she checked under the small cot and found a heavy green duffel bag. She dragged the duffel bag out and examined the contents. "Clothes, but not hunting clothes, just like I thought."

"I don't understand," Andrew said, watching Sarah hold up an expensive green cashmere sweater.

"I do," Amanda said in a quick voice. "Milton said he noticed some clothes were missing from Mr. Hopski's closet, right?" she asked Sarah.

Sarah nodded her head. "I doubt a man like Mr. Hopski would keep his broken-in hunting clothes in his main closet," Sarah explained. She walked back to the bed and retrieved two pairs of fine, leather walking boots. The boots were worn in. "I bet if we examine the clothes Mr. Hopski was found dead in we would find out those clothes were brand new. A seasoned hunter like Mr. Hopski, who doesn't seem to be a hunter after all, would have his own style of hunting clothes, worn-in and smelling like the land itself."

"Hey, that's right," Andrew said. "My hunting outfit is older than my son." Andrew looked at the front door. "Sarah, we've got a lot of paths to explore when we get back to town."

"Let's go explore the airfield first," Sarah said in a patient voice.

"I guess Mr. Hopski didn't hate to fly after all," Amanda told Sarah as she followed her back outside.

"No, I guess not," Sarah agreed, walking around the cabin and making her way into the open field that was more mud than grass. Andrew brought up the rear, keeping an eye out for bears. "We need to examine the north part of this field. That's the only place a small aircraft could touch down, based on the trees around the field. Come on."

Amanda followed Sarah to the front of the field, keeping her eyes on the ground. It wasn't long before she spotted fresh wheel tracks. "Sarah, look at this!" Amanda pointed down to the ground.

Sarah bent down and moved some grass away. "Good going," she congratulated Amanda. "Andrew, look at this." Andrew ran over to Sarah, bent down, and studied the wheel tracks. "Looks like someone has been here recently."

"I'd say maybe...a week ago, maybe two," Andrew suggested, "judging from the tracks."

"Maybe just long enough to move a body," Sarah pointed out. "Come on, we better get back to town."

"Yep," Andrew said and checked his rifle, "we got a long walk ahead of us, too. Brace yourself, ladies, you're likely to end up with sore feet before the day is over."

Amanda sighed. "My hubby's bell doesn't sound half bad right about now," she told Sarah.

Sarah imagined Amanda's warm, cozy cabin. She saw the two of them sitting in Amanda's kitchen sipping coffee, nibbling hot cinnamon buns, talking about shopping trips, and worrying about absolutely nothing. But she had a job to do, a killer to catch, and justice to serve. "Let's get walking, June Bug."

Amanda nodded her head and took her middle spot as Sarah moved back to the rear. "Ready, Andrew," Sarah called out. Andrew pointed into the woods and they got moving.

Three hours later, Andrew wearily trudged back up to his truck, climbed into the driver's seat, and waited for Sarah and Amanda. Once Sarah and Amanda were safely tucked into the cab, he turned his truck around and started easing back down the old Snow Bear Trail toward town. They were all tired and barely spoke on the drive back. Sarah could feel the rope and the journal glowing like hot coals in the pockets of her rain jacket.

As soon as they pulled into town and walked into the police station, Andrew was met by a very angry Natalie Hopski who sat in his office. "I've been waiting for hours," she snapped.

Andrew eased into his office, walked over to his desk, and sat down. Sarah and Amanda had stopped outside in the hallway when they heard her voice. They listened, allowing Natalie to believe Andrew was alone. "I've been out on an investigation, Ms. Hopski," Andrew replied. "That's not against the law, is it?"

"Don't get smart with me!" Natalie pounced on Andrew. "Has the autopsy report on my father come back yet?"

"No," Andrew said, nearly going blind from fatigue and blinking at the sight of the green and orange striped dress Natalie was wearing. "I can make a call to the coroner and find out where he's at."

"You do that!"

Andrew didn't like Natalie and after nearly twenty-four hours without more than four hours of sleep, he decided that the time for being polite was over. "Ms. Hopski, I'm not making a single call until you learn to speak to an officer of the law with respect. If you refuse, you can remove yourself from my office. Do I make myself clear?"

"Wow," Amanda whispered, "Andrew stopped being polite. Go, Andrew."

"Go, Andrew," Sarah cheered in a low voice.

Natalie's face snarled up into a knot. "Listen to me—"

"No, you listen to me, Ms. Hopski. This department is doing all that it can to make sure your father receives the best from us. It's one thing for a man to be found dead, and it's another thing to rush his autopsy. Around here, lady, we respect those who have gone on before us. Understand?"

"My lawyer is going to have your job!" Natalie yelled and stormed up to her feet.

"He's more than welcome to have it," Andrew said in a calm but weary voice, "but I doubt he'll take it. I'll turn over my badge when I choose to, and that won't be for a good many years yet."

"We'll see about that," Natalie hissed.

Sarah grabbed Amanda's hand and ran her into the women's bathroom just as Natalie burst out of Andrew's office. Natalie huffed at the two police officers staring at her in the lobby and made her way outside. "Well, let's not leave Andrew alone," Sarah said and hurried out of the bathroom and into Andrew's office. She found Andrew making a call. Andrew raised a calm hand at her. Sarah nodded and sat down with Amanda.

Andrew was evidently on the phone with the coroner. "Any update on Mr. Hopski? ...Yeah...I see... Yeah, still waiting on the labs and then you'll bring the official report down... Is that your final opinion? ...Sure...I understand. Yes sir, I'll give my wife your best. Thanks a lot." Andrew hung up the phone. He looked at Sarah and Amanda with sober eyes. "Our coroner believes Mr. Hopski died due to extreme exposure to the elements."

Sarah shook her head. "So much for my theories."

"But," Andrew added, "his examination lab is, well, very small, you know. With the evidence we gathered today I can request Mr. Hopski be sent to the main crime lab in Anchorage for a second autopsy. Also, the lab results haven't come back yet, so there could still be something hidden under the dirt."

"Let's hope so," Sarah said in an urgent voice. "And right now, we need time." Sarah looked at the office door. "We need time to set a trap."

"I'll make the call, then."

"And you and I," Sarah told Amanda, standing up, "are

going to go get some lunch. Andrew, we'll bring you back a burger plate." Andrew waved his hand at Sarah and grabbed his phone. "Let's go, Amanda."

Amanda followed Sarah out of Andrew's office and bumped right into Chet and Milton. Milton was wearing another pinstripe suit, cream with tiny black stripes this time, that made him look like an extra from a B-movie about to stroll down a boardwalk. Chet, on the other hand, was more soberly dressed in a plain gray t-shirt over a pair of tan pants. The man looked worried and upset. "Chet?" Sarah asked, concerned.

"Doll face," Milton said and tipped his fedora hat, "we need to talk, and talk now."

"What's wrong?" Sarah demanded.

Milton looked up at his brother. "Should I tell her or you?" he asked in a quiet voice. Sarah could see that he was sweating a little bit.

"You tell her," Chet said and looked down at his meaty hands. "I don't think I can."

"What is it?" Sarah said.

"Well," Milton swallowed, "it's Charlene, you see." Milton looked down at his feet. "She's...well..."

"What?" Sarah asked.

"She's kinda...dead," Milton confessed.

Sarah almost didn't believe her ears, and simply waited for him to go on. He seemed to cringe, as if waiting for Sarah to tear into him. "We didn't kill her, honest. Chet and me, we just wanted to talk to her, so we went to her room after breakfast. We found her door smashed open and when we walked into her room we found..." Milton looked up at Sarah with sorrowful eyes. "Charlene...well, she had a...a rope around her neck. Enough said."

"We closed the door and called you but you weren't here. So, we drove here and waited," Chet explained. "But then we saw Natalie drive up and come inside. All we could do was wait inside."

"Why didn't you tell the officers that were here?" Sarah begged.

"Because we were too scared to," Chet admitted. "We trust you...Sarah...and we trust Amanda." Chet lifted his eyes and looked into Sarah's face with honesty and desperation. "We didn't kill Charlene."

"But this..." Milton reached into her pocket and pulled out a note, "says we did." Milton handed the note to Sarah.

Sarah opened the note and read it. "To whoever may find this: Milton and Chet have threatened to kill me. If I am found dead I hope this note convicts my killers." Sarah looked at Milton. "Where did you find this note?"

"On Charlene's bed," Chet explained. "Don't make sense for that woman to leave a note like that lying around if we killed her, does it?"

"I mean, what does Charlene take us for, idiots? What does she think, we would kill her and just leave her note out in the open for the fuzz to find?" Milton shook his head with disgust.

"Maybe Natalie is getting desperate," Sarah explained. She looked over her shoulder at Andrew's office door. "Come on, guys, we have to speak with Andrew."

"So much for food," Amanda sighed. "Chet, Milton, maybe you boys can treat a hungry girl to dinner later."

Chet and Milton weren't in the mood to joke. They were worried sick as they followed the two women into Andrew's office.

Outside, Natalie Hopski's car sped away, unaware that she had just narrowly missed crossing paths with Chet and Milton in the hallway of the police station. If she had seen them, she might have learned that her brothers had found Charlene's body. As far as she knew, Charlene's body still remained undiscovered. What she also didn't know was that the door to Charlene's room had been left open instead of fully closed. "I'll kill them all," Natalie promised herself as she sped back to the lodge, determined to use Charlene's death to destroy Chet and Milton and claim her father's fortune all for herself. "I'll kill them all and show them just how dangerous crossing Natalie Hopski is."

chapter six

Andrew shoved his hands down into the pockets of his jeans. "Fellas, you should have let one of my guys know," he said in an upset voice. "By not doing so...well, it doesn't make you look good."

"We were scared," Milton repeated apologetically. He took a brown paper cup full of coffee from Amanda and took a sip. "We knew Natalie killed Charlene and she might come for us next."

"I'm not scared of her," Chet said in a flat voice. His face was steady but his eyes were worried. He looked up at Sarah. "We didn't kill Charlene, Sarah."

"I know," Sarah said and offered Chet a supportive smile. They had just sat through Andrew's process of taking their statements, a tiring process that seemed to turn up nothing much helpful. She decided to take a new track. She held up Mr. Hopski's journal. "Guys, I've spent the last two hours reading this journal. There are some very interesting entries in this journal that prove, at least to me, that your father was very worried about Natalie, if not downright scared of her." She briefly went over some of the more shocking revelations in the early entries.

"So Pop never went hunting, ever?" Milton asked in a

shocked voice. "Pop just came up here to the woods and hid out in a cabin?"

"A cabin he built for his wife after World War II. You might not know it, but your mother was from this part of the country," Sarah explained. "Your father loved your mother more than pen can describe on paper."

"We know that," Chet assured Sarah.

"Here," Amanda told Chet and handed him a cup of coffee. "Hot coffee always helps."

Chet took the cup of coffee from Amanda and took a sip. His eyes became thoughtful. "What did Daddy say about Natalie?" he asked Sarah.

Sarah leaned back against Andrew's desk and listened to a strong wind howl outside. A powerful spring storm was moving in over Snow Falls. The outside sky was low, dark and ominous. "Mr. Hopski had concerns that Natalie did push your mother to her death," Sarah explained in a sad voice. "He could never bring himself to speak his thoughts outright, but deep down in his heart, he knew the truth."

"So Pop wasn't blind after all," Milton stated in a half-relieved voice. "Pop wasn't a stupid fella."

"No, he wasn't," Sarah agreed. She opened the journal and cleared her throat. "But he was scared. Listen to this entry from last year, right before he left for Alaska." Sarah cleared her throat again. "I'm leaving for the cabin, this time to die. I know Natalie is out to kill me. I would rather die at the cabin where I can rest in the memory of my wife than die in this awful city where my daughter will never let me rest." Sarah closed the journal. "There is enough in this journal to force Natalie into a very tight corner. However, a team of lawyers would chew through the journal in a minute, claiming the writing was by a man suffering from bipolar depression. The journal by itself is not enough. Natalie would eventually slip through our fingers. We don't want that to happen."

Andrew stood up from behind his desk. "I have two dead

bodies in my town, Sarah. It won't be long before the state police start poking their noses into our town, sniffing around for answers." Andrew drew in a deep breath. "Guys, I'm afraid I'm going to have to place you both under protective custody for the time being. I'm not arresting you, but I do need to protect you from Natalie. Not to mention, the note Charlene Nelton left behind points a direct finger at the both of you. And because you didn't report the death immediately and decided to wait…well, it casts suspicion into your corner. As it stands, you could have killed Charlene Nelton and now be trying to pin the murder on your sister."

"What?" Milton protested. "You heard what Pop wrote in his journal, you crummy cop! We didn't kill that scarecrow Charlene any more than you did!"

"I know that," Andrew stated in a calm voice, "but the law is the law and I have my job to do. If you're innocent, let the rest of this investigation bear that out. Besides," he added, "I don't want any more dead bodies in my town. Protective custody is the best I can do for the time being."

"Andrew is right," Sarah said in a reluctant voice. "I don't feel that Natalie is working alone and—"

The phone on Andrew's desk rang. "Just a second," Andrew said and answered the call. Sarah waited. Amanda walked over to Milton and Chet and patted their shoulders in a show of support. "Okay, thanks a lot," Andrew said and hung up the phone. "That was the coroner. He's bringing over the official report."

Sarah examined Andrew's face. "But—?" she prompted.

"There were heavy traces of sedatives in Mr. Hopski's blood along with a strong hallucinogen," Andrew explained. "But no traces of any kind of medication that might treat depression. Seems like there was something under the dirt, after all."

Sarah focused on Chet's face. The poor man's jowl dropped with sadness. "Poor Daddy was killed, just like

Momma," he whispered. A tear dropped from his eye. Milton sat stunned.

Sarah sighed. What could she say? Before she could say anything, the phone rang again. Andrew answered the call. "Hello? No, I understand… Oh, is that so? Thanks. Yeah, the older we get the more we seem to forget. Thanks for calling me back," Andrew said and ended the call. He looked at Sarah. "That was the coroner again. He forgot to tell me that the hair sample we found on the rope matches to Mr. Hopski."

Sarah wasn't surprised by the results. "Chet, Milton, I need to look at Mr. Hopski's will. My gut is telling me that some recent changes might have been made."

"Phil Cohen is Pop's lawyer," Milton told Sarah. "Phil is a good guy, old like Pop was… kinda rough and gruff, but he cares. Why?"

Sarah opened the journal in her hands again just as thunder exploded outside and shook the office. "Listen to this entry." Sarah looked at the downpour outside the office window. "I changed my will. If I am found to be murdered, my money goes straight to my two sons, Chet and Milton. Natalie found out about the change and became furious with me. I fear she will now try to end my life. I will be leaving for my cabin soon in an attempt to hide from her." Sarah looked up to see the look of horror on Milton's face and sorrow on Chet's face. "Charlene has been spending a lot of time with Natalie. I fear I know the reason. By now, Natalie must have informed Charlene I changed the terms and conditions in my will. I'm scared for my life."

"Poor Daddy," Chet said. He looked up guiltily and said, "We didn't know about the will, honest."

"I believe you," Sarah promised Chet.

"What do you think this means?" Milton asked Sarah in an upset voice. "My mind is racing, I can't think. But a woman like you must have a theory."

"I think your father was drugged and forced to change his will."

"The hallucinogenic drug," Amanda said.

Sarah nodded her head. "After that he was given sedatives, tied up, and led out into the woods and left for dead. Later, after he died, his body was moved to the old Snow Bear Trail where it would eventually be discovered, once spring arrived. Mr. Hopski's body was found in a way that made it appear he became lost and died of exposure to the elements."

Amanda balled her hands into two tight fists. "Oh, someone is going down," she promised. "And that someone is Natalie Hopski."

"Natalie Hopski wasn't working alone," Sarah pointed out. She rubbed her chin. "I'm thinking Natalie was setting Charlene up to take the fall, but for some reason, Charlene became a threat to Natalie's plan, which forced Natalie to kill her." Sarah continued to think through the theory. "I wonder what Charlene found out? No matter, what we have to focus on right now is Natalie Hopski."

Amanda sat down next to Sarah, lost in thought. "The handwriting on the note Chet and Milton found matches Charlene's handwriting, right? So could she have also been pumped full of a hallucinogenic drug?"

"Possible," Sarah admitted. "The coroner will tell us in time. But my professional opinion is, yes, Charlene Nelton was given the same drug as Mr. Hopski."

Andrew shook his head. "Sarah, this isn't good."

"No, it's not," Chet spoke in a worried voice. "I have something to confess."

"Yes?" Sarah asked, surprised to hear him pipe up so suddenly.

"My wife takes sedatives," Chet said. He looked at Milton with worried eyes.

"Tell them," Milton sighed heavily.

"I can't," Chet said and shook his head. He looked down at his meaty hands and grew silent.

"Chet, please," Sarah pleaded.

"Chet, should I tell them?" Milton asked in a sad voice. "I think they ought to know." Chet reluctantly nodded his head yes. Milton drew in a deep breath and steadied his mind. "Teresa, Chet's wife, she works at one of them drug rehab centers, you know. She was a big druggie herself when she was young and eventually got clean, went back to school and got her degree in counseling. She started working at...what's the name of the place...oh yeah...Sunshine Rehab. I know, that's a really lame name for a drug rehab place, but you know how southern California is."

"I know," Sarah promised Milton.

"Anyways," Milton paused long enough to listen to the sky open outside as a raging rain began to fall. "Teresa was fired from her job last year. It seems...well, she was accused of...well, maybe she had a relapse," Milton said, "though she denied it up and down." He shook his head sadly. "Her supervisor said a whole lot of drugs went missing from the rehab center shortly before Teresa was fired."

"Hallucinogenic drugs?" Sarah asked pointedly.

"Who knows?" Milton shrugged his shoulders.

"Yes," Chet said and raised his eyes. "Sunshine Rehab had to confiscate illegal drugs from the patients all the time. And she knew—" he stopped, unable to continue.

"She knew where the confiscated drugs were stored," Milton finished for Chet. "She was in charge of them, in fact. So yeah, doll face, hallucinogenic drugs could have been among what was stolen."

"By my wife," Chet said in a miserable voice.

"But why would your wife want to help kill your father?" Amanda asked Chet. Chet did not meet her eyes. His brother was silent, too. It was a tense moment.

Milton only looked down at his cup of coffee. "I always suspected, but I never said a word," he said quietly.

Sarah turned to look at Amanda and then at Andrew. Andrew nodded his head. "Milton, what did you suspect, exactly?"

The office grew silent again. The sound of the heavy rain falling outside filled the silence expectantly, like a crowd staring at something dangerous. Sarah waited patiently for Milton to speak, even though her gut knew what words the man was going to relay to everyone. Still, Sarah knew not to push him and to let the man speak at his own pace. After all, she reminded herself, Milton and Chet were both dealing with the loss of a father they loved very much.

As a cop, it was sometimes too easy to press a person for answers and forget the person had emotions and thoughts of their own that mattered. In the world of cops versus civilians, the cops had a tendency to become impersonal and simply focus on the case at hand, forgetting that their sole purpose was to Protect and Defend and not Control and Conquer. Being a cop was a risky business that meant dealing with dangerous people and sometimes it was difficult to remember how vulnerable victims truly were. And Milton and Chet were not bad guys. They were victims.

Milton finally raised his eyes and looked up into Sarah's sweet and caring face. "I always kinda figured Teresa and Natalie favored each other, that's all. As a coincidence. I mean, their looks. What were the odds of them actually being sisters?" He swallowed nervously and looked over at his brother, but Chet would not meet Milton's eyes. Milton continued. "But over time, I started to notice that they, well, had some of the same character traits, you know... Teresa wasn't as mean as Natalie was, no way, but her eyes...after a while, they grew dark." Milton looked at Chet again. "Please don't be mad at me."

"I'm not mad at you," Chet promised his brother, his eyes

still downcast. "How can I be? I...agree with you," he said in a tormented voice. "But Teresa was supposed to love me. We said our vows. For better or for worse. I thought she would stand by me...the way I always stood by her."

Sarah's heart broke anew. "I'll run a check and see if Natalie had any biological siblings," Sarah promised. "If your hunch is correct, we may have found the source of the hallucinogens."

"I wish I was wrong," Milton replied miserably. "All I ever wanted was for my brother to be happy. I can run through a passel of wives and have them dump me and be okay with that. I have thick skin. But Chet, well, he's tender-hearted and gets his feelings hurt real easy." Milton rubbed Chet's shoulder. "We could be wrong about Teresa."

"We're not," Chet replied to Milton woodenly. He looked up at Sarah. "I sensed the change in my wife. I knew her heart turned bad. I didn't say anything when she was fired from her job at the rehab clinic. I didn't say anything when she started coming home late. I didn't say anything when she stayed gone for days at a time. I was afraid to lose her. Now, I've lost her altogether." Chet stood up and walked out of the office, despondent.

"Let him go," Andrew said quietly, "I doubt he'll try and make a run for it."

"I'll go check on him," Milton said and excused himself.

Andrew waited until Milton left his office before speaking. "It's still a mighty hard task for two women to handle alone," he pointed out. "Even two big and strong women."

"I agree," Sarah said. Sarah and Andrew exchanged a worried look. Sarah patted Amanda's hand. "Let's go down to the lodge and look around and ask some questions."

"Okay," Amanda said and walked over to the office door. She turned and looked at Andrew's worried face. "You two think there's a third person, don't you? A man."

"Possibly," Sarah said. "Andrew, run a check on Teresa

and Natalie. See if they were listed as siblings in the foster care system – but also check and see if there were any other biological brothers and sisters. I think the pieces are starting to come together."

"Will do," Andrew promised and watched Sarah and Amanda leave his office and enter a dark storm.

Shelly Brights stood up from behind the polished wooden counter and yawned. As pretty as she was, she was young enough that she hadn't yet learned how to keep the snotty, bored look off her face. "More cops," she moaned, and put down her novel.

Sarah walked across the shiny hardwood floor of the lodge's lobby. It smelled of Pine-Sol, and she looked around at the cozy lounge area with its two green armchairs, a wooden shelf lined with interesting mysteries, and an inviting coffee bar filled with donuts and pastries. But the cozy lodge seemed otherwise deserted.

"What can I do for you?" Shelly asked in a put-upon voice as she smoothed back her long blond hair. "This is just terrible for business; my parents are going to be so mad when they get back. They leave me alone to manage the lodge for a week and look what happens – a murder." Shelly shook her head. "I haven't sold a room all day."

"Honey," Amanda said and pointed to the dark storm outside, "cut the attitude, okay? This is a crime scene, but with a storm like this there's not going to be a single tourist looking for a room anyway."

Shelly watched as Amanda shook rain from her white umbrella. "Don't wet my floor," she complained.

Sarah sighed and braced herself. She loved the residents of her new town, even though some were very rough around the edges. "Where were you last night?" she asked, skipping any pleasantries.

Shelly tossed a thumb at a door behind her. "In the managers' apartment where we live, where else?" she said in a bored voice. "At nine sharp I closed the lobby, cooked myself a late dinner, watched a few reruns and went to bed."

Sarah searched the lobby for any security cameras and came up empty. "No security cameras?" she asked.

"Why should there be?" Shelly asked. "Just in case you haven't noticed, we live in the middle of nowhere with a bunch of bears. If anyone is pathetic enough to want to rob me for the twenty-five dollars I have in my cash drawer, then let them be my guest." Shelly flicked a piece of lint off the blue sweater she was wearing. "Any more questions?"

"Where do you keep the keys to the rooms?" Sarah asked.

Shelly rolled her eyes. She walked over to a metal box on a nearby desk and dumped it unceremoniously on the front counter in front of Sarah. "In the Key Box," she said and opened it with a key she fished out of her pocket. Sarah looked into the box and saw a row of keys fastened to numbered hooks, plus a mess of loose keys and rusty old keyrings at the bottom of the box. She wordlessly gave Shelly a look, and the young woman snapped the box shut defensively. "Well, this isn't a five-star hotel. What did you expect, electronic key cards?"

"Maybe not," Amanda said, "but your parents do a very fine job here. This place is beautifully rustic and the inside is almost romantic. You should be proud of your parents' accomplishments."

Shelly rolled her eyes. "I'll be proud of my own accomplishments after I ditch this town and leave for college and become a doctor."

Amanda winced. "You might want to work on your bedside manner, love."

"Whatever," Shelly said and slammed the box back down

onto the desk behind her. "Any more questions?"

"Did you see Natalie return to her room before you closed the lobby down?" Sarah asked.

"Nope," Shelly said and yawned. "I saw them leave but not return."

"Okay," Sarah said and pointed to a set of stairs leading up to the second floor, "let's go take a look at Charlene's room."

"Don't make a mess. The cops already came and taped it all off. My parents are returning back from Seattle tonight," Shelly pleaded with Sarah.

Amanda shook her head at Shelly and followed Sarah up the stairs and down a cozy carpeted hallway. They stopped at room number eight. Yellow police tape was stretched across the door. Sarah ducked under the tape and entered the room. All of Charlene's personal belongings had been removed and taken down to the police station, but Sarah figured the killers had removed any other damaging evidence from the room long before Andrew and his crime scene team had arrived. "We should have accompanied Andrew to the lodge and investigated the room earlier," Sarah griped.

"But Milton and Chet were really upset and neither of us wanted to leave them," Amanda reminded Sarah. Sarah was inspecting the king-sized bed covered in a green and brown quilt. Amanda glanced up and saw the hand-carved beams that crossed the ceiling. A shiver worked its way down her spine. "I'm just glad I didn't see the body," she said.

Sarah ran her finger across the foot of the bed and looked around. The room was of comfortable size, resembling the lobby in style, simple but rustic. "Chet, Milton, Natalie, and Charlene were the only guests staying here," she said. "Last night, Chet and Milton were with us...so Natalie would have had the perfect chance to carry out a murder."

Amanda folded her arms. "Love, what exactly are we looking for?" she asked.

"Not something with our eyes, but with our noses. Have you noticed that Natalie wears a very distinct perfume?" Sarah asked. "The perfume is barely noticeable, but very distinct."

"You mean the skunk spray I smelled on her. I thought it was just the woman's bad breath?" Amanda replied, making a face.

Sarah smelled the air. She could see that someone would have had to stand on the bed to reach the ceiling beams. She bent down to the quilt and her nose caught a faint scent of Natalie's perfume. "Natalie was in this room," she assured Amanda. "Now, imagine for a moment you want to kill someone but don't want your victim putting up a fight. What steps would you take to subdue that person?"

Amanda listened to the heavy rain falling outside as she considered Sarah's question. "Sedatives?" she said.

"Yes, but," Sarah explained, "that person isn't going to be drugged without putting up a fight. Charlene Nelton was lured away from the lodge, drugged, brought back, and hung." Sarah studied the empty room. "Right now, Natalie Hopski is under lockdown in her room. Did you notice how her attitude changed when she was brought down to the police station and informed that Charlene Nelton was dead? She suddenly became very afraid of Milton and Chet. All an act of course, but very convincing."

"She wants poor Milton and Chet to take the fall for Charlene's death," Amanda said in an angry voice. "I saw how that bat changed her tone from evil to frightened in a blink of an eye. She practically begged for Andrew to lock her in her room. For her own protection, of course."

"Of course," Sarah said. "It seems like Natalie Hopski had a deadly plan formed in her twisted mind long before she left Los Angeles and traveled to our little town, June Bug." Sarah continued to search the room with skilled eyes. "But Natalie Hopski isn't as brilliant as she believes. Mr. Hopski's journal is going to be the one item that takes that woman down and throws her into prison."

Amanda caught a certain tone in Sarah's voice that made her ears prick up. Sarah was setting a trap, because perhaps Natalie Hopski was listening. Sarah looked at Amanda and pointed to the beautiful hand-carved lamp sitting on a night stand beside the bed. She walked over to the lamp, bent down, and looked up into its pink lamp shade. And there, sitting tucked inside the lamp, was a tiny, black listening device. Amanda hurried over to the lamp, knelt down, and spotted it. Sarah placed a finger to her lips and backed away from the lamp. "We're going to focus on the autopsy report for now. The results clearly show Mr. Hopski had been drugged. But even with that evidence, Natalie could still slip through our hands. Mr. Hopski's journal is the hidden trap that's going to catch that woman."

"What if she tries to slip town on us?" Amanda asked, playing along.

"She won't. Natalie Hopski wants her daddy's money, June Bug," Sarah stated in an important voice. "As long as there is a dark cloud hanging over her head, she'll stick around. My guess is she's going to request Mr. Hopski's body be sent to another coroner, possibly someone who will come to a different conclusion than ours. Then she can challenge it in court."

"Can she do that?" Amanda asked.

"Money talks," Sarah replied in a serious voice. "Mr. Hopski's journal is our secret weapon. But for now, we're going to have to play it easy and see if Natalie slips up. It'll help our case if we can stick more on her than the words Mr. Hopski wrote in his journal. It's a good thing I've hidden the journal for safe keeping." Sarah looked around the room again. "Natalie Hopski was in this room, but there's no way to prove it. I guess we've hit a dead end here. Let's get a bite to eat at the diner. I'm starved."

Amanda followed Sarah out of the room and back down into the lobby. Shelly was reading a magazine and ignored their presence. "Let us know if Natalie Hopski leaves her room," Sarah instructed Shelly. Shelly waved a bored hand in the air. "Come on, June Bug."

Amanda walked out into the pouring rain, opened her umbrella, stuck it up over her head and said: "The day has really turned dark."

Sarah stepped under the umbrella. As she did, thunder erupted and shook the ground. Two police officers waved from their squad car parked in front of the lobby. Sarah didn't blame them. The day was dark and very stormy, better to ride it out from inside the squad car instead of stand in front of the lobby doors. The winds were gusting and forcing trees to bend more than they wanted to while blowing rain across the gravel parking lot at each bluster of high speed. "It's going to turn much darker," Sarah promised Amanda. "We set a trap for Natalie. The woman is surely going to take the bait. How and when? That's the question."

"I just feel so awful for Milton and Chet. I know Milton is a little flirt, but he's harmless. And all Chet wants is for a woman to love him." Amanda stared into the storm. "It's true what they say, isn't it? Money can't buy love."

"Love needs love," Sarah agreed and walked Amanda to her truck. "Let's go get a bite to eat. My stomach is empty."

"Sure, love."

Sarah drove Amanda to the diner, parked, and they hurried inside. The diner was almost empty except for two old men sitting in a booth, sipping coffee, trading war stories. "Rain has run my customers off," Anne told Sarah and Amanda. "Sit where you want, ladies. I'll go get you some coffee."

"And two burger plates, please," Amanda called after Anne.

"You're getting chicken and dumplings," Anne informed

Amanda in a tough but motherly voice. Amanda grinned. She liked Anne a lot.

Sarah plopped down in a booth near the front door and rubbed her legs. "My feet are killing me. I was expecting to do quite a bit of walking today, but my legs sure weren't prepared."

"Being stuck inside all winter takes its toll," Amanda told Sarah and removed her rain jacket. "My legs, love, feel like they're on fire." Amanda sighed. "I wish I had a bell to ring."

"You're doing great. You always do, June Bug," Sarah told Amanda with love. "I know it was scary being so far out in the woods today. After Andrew scared off the bear, it took everything inside of my heart not to turn around and run back to my cabin at a very high speed."

"Oh, it was scary, wasn't it," Amanda said in a hushed voice, remembering the moment. "I can't imagine being lost out in the wilderness alone, without shelter, food, or water..." Amanda stopped talking. She looked into Sarah's eyes. "Oh, I see. You're very clever."

"I want you to think as Mr. Hopski might have been thinking," Sarah affirmed with a grin. "Think about it, June Bug. His body was too neat and orderly for someone who had been lost out in the woods. When panic sets in, a person becomes very messy. Mr. Hopski's body was found too close to a trail to be just mere coincidence. At first, I thought the man must have been familiar with this area, but even that theory didn't sit well with me." Sarah removed her rain jacket and set it down next to her. "I began asking myself questions...such as where was Mr. Hopski's hunting cabin? Was he alone? Why did he come to Alaska to hunt during the winter season? Simply finding a hunter frozen to death doesn't mean the death is accidental. Of course, it could have been, but a good detective rules out all suspicions before drawing a final conclusion."

"When Natalie arrived, you knew Mr. Hopski had been

murdered, didn't you? While Andrew and I were laughing, you were doing your job."

"Natalie Hopski and Charlene Nelton struck a bad feeling in my heart, yes," Sarah confirmed. "June Bug, being a cop isn't easy. We dealt with some pretty dangerous people last winter. You held your head high above the water, too. So don't knock yourself for splitting a gut."

"Oh, I'm not," Amanda sighed. "I just feel so bad for Milton and Chet. Those poor dears. What are they going to do, love? Chet will never trust a living soul ever again. And Milton, he's so sweet and so lonely. He just...comes on a bit too flirty." Amanda rested her chin on the palms of her hands. "I wish there was something we could do for them."

"Pray," Sarah smiled.

"I have," Amanda promised. She sighed again. "They'll go back to Los Angeles and live out their lives rich, but lonely and sad. Chet will probably grow bitter and angry and Milton will continue chasing empty relationships that will end in divorce."

Sarah knew Amanda was speaking the truth. But what could she do? Ask Milton and Chet to relocate to a small town in Alaska and settle down with the bears? Milton needed the beach and Chet wasn't exactly a skilled outdoorsman. "Those two will have to learn that when life gives you hard knocks, you just have to take it, stand back up, and move on with your life. If they choose to be bitter, well...that's a choice. Not fate."

Amanda gave Sarah a sad face. "Some people aren't as strong as you, Los Angeles. I'm one of them. If Jack ever divorced me, my life would be shattered into a million little pieces. I would never be able to live whole again."

Sarah patted Amanda's hand reassuringly and looked out into the dark rain. They continued to chat as they waited for their food, but Sarah felt uneasy knowing that they were just waiting for Natalie Hopski to take the bait and show up.

chapter seven

When Natalie strolled into the diner, her eyes were narrowed with suspicion. She spotted Sarah and Amanda sitting close to the front door and quickly closed her umbrella, dumping rain messily all over the floor. Sarah took a sip of coffee and waited for her to approach the booth. "Right on time," she whispered.

Amanda took a sip of coffee and watched Sarah's eyes. "Get her, tiger," she grinned.

As she crossed the short distance to them, Natalie dropped her calculating look and widened her eyes in fake fear. "I decided to risk leaving my room. I can't very well starve to death, can I?" she asked.

Sarah looked up at Natalie. The woman was wearing the ugliest purple and pink rain jacket she had ever seen in her life, but she tried to ignore that. "The police station would have arranged to bring you your meals if you're concerned about your safety, Ms. Hopski. And in this weather, maybe you should have called us." Sarah motioned to the raging storm outside.

Natalie glanced back at the front door. "Well," she said, adding a note of fake courage to her voice, "I don't like living in fear. I consider myself an independent woman, Detective

Garland. Much like yourself." Natalie looked down at Sarah. "I take it my two brothers are now under arrest?" she asked in a hopeful voice.

"For now," Sarah replied, omitting the detail that they were in protective custody, allowing Natalie to believe she was in control of the situation. "However, I do not believe your brothers are guilty. I believe Mr. Hopski was killed and the same person who killed him is now attempting to frame your brothers."

"Well," Natalie said in a pinched, displeased voice, "a note written in the dead woman's own handwriting claiming my brothers are the killers will be enough to convince any jury."

"A bought jury, perhaps," Sarah replied and locked eyes with Natalie. "I don't like you, Ms. Hopski. You're an awful woman who makes my stomach turn. I also believe you are involved in the killing of Mr. Hopski and the death of Charlene Nelton and I intend to prove that. For now, I have only my gut feeling to go by and no substantial, concrete evidence. But I will. In the meantime, if you leave town, I will place a warrant out for your arrest quicker than you can blink an eye."

"Oh, don't worry about that," Natalie hissed at Sarah, "I have no intention of leaving this miserable little town until I have received the justice I deserve and you, Detective Garland, receive exactly what you deserve."

"Is that a threat?" Sarah asked levelly, taking a calm sip of her coffee.

Natalie narrowed her eyes. "Nobody crosses Natalie Hopski and wins," she warned Sarah. "And as far as you believing I killed my miserable old father and his shrew of a wife, well, you can try to prove it, but you will fail."

"I may have a hidden weapon," Sarah promised. "Arrogant confidence is what always destroys a killer."

Natalie gritted her teeth. "You're a problem that I will deal with...in my own way," she whispered and pointed an ugly finger at Amanda. "You and your snotty little friend."

Amanda looked up into Natalie's mocking face and then stood up from the booth. "Take your best shot, you disgusting bully," she said and took an aggressive step towards Natalie. Natalie stumbled back, tripped over her own feet, and crashed backward onto the floor.

Despite her awkward fall, Natalie seemed undaunted. Her face twisted with evil as she sneered up at Amanda, "Is that all you've got? You're pathetic."

Amanda was on the older woman before Sarah could even blink. "Amanda!" she yelled, shocked that her best friend had turned violent.

Amanda ignored Sarah's pleas and grabbed Natalie around her thick neck, leaning into her as hard as she could. She had had enough of the likes of Natalie Hopski. Sure, Amanda thought blindly as she began to squeeze into the flesh of the older woman's neck. She was going to end up in the slammer for assault, but so what? She would spend the night in jail with a smile on her face. "You will learn some manners, you ugly, disgusting bully!" Amanda gritted out between clenched teeth, leaning close to Natalie's face.

Sarah jumped to her feet, ran to Amanda, and pulled her best friend off of Natalie, who coughed hoarsely and flailed away from her attacker. "Oh, let me at her! Let me at her!" Amanda demanded and tried to break free from Sarah's grip. "I'll rip her hair out!"

Natalie, in a state of fright and shock, coughed and felt blood trickling from her mouth. "Arrest her at once!" she ordered as soon as her shock wore off. "Arrest that...vermin at once!"

"Vermin? Oh, let me at her!" Amanda screamed and reached out her hands toward Natalie. Natalie flinched, crawled to her feet, and backed away from Amanda. "Get back here, you overgrown ogre!"

"How dare you!"

Sarah held Amanda back. She wasn't about to arrest her best friend, yet she couldn't let Amanda tear Natalie Hopski to shreds, either. "Cool down, girl," Sarah begged.

"Arrest her!" Natalie demanded. She pointed at the two old men sitting close by. "You saw that woman attack me, didn't you?"

The two old men shook their heads no, hesitant to be dragged into the fray. "We didn't see anything," said one man quietly, and they both went back to their coffee.

"You," Natalie said to Sarah, as she wiped blood from her lips again, "you saw your friend attack me."

"I saw you provoke a fight," Sarah corrected Natalie. "You made a threat and my friend reacted."

"I was...speaking about a legal threat," Natalie said with indignation. "Hardly an incitement to violence," she sniffed.

"You're lying through your teeth," Amanda snarled. "Anytime you want more of me, you just let me know and we'll go at it again. Now get out of here!"

"My lawyer is going to eat you alive!" Natalie yelled at Amanda.

"Not if you go to prison first!" Amanda shot back. "Don't leave town because the firework show is about to start."

"You can count on it!" Natalie hissed at Amanda and pointed at Sarah. "The victory is mine, detective. You messed with the wrong woman."

"I'm not so sure," Sarah promised Natalie. It was time to sweeten the trap. "Today I found your father's hunting cabin and a journal—" she stopped herself, as if realizing she had said too much. She immediately saw Natalie's eyes blaze up in curiosity. The prey had entered the trap. "Uh, that is, I found a very important piece of evidence. But in the woods we also found a bit of rope with a hair attached to it that came from Mr. Hopski's body." Sarah let go of Amanda's arms. "The trek out to the cabin took a few hours, but we found the cabin...and the small air strip behind the cabin. What we didn't find was your late father's green Subaru. According to your brothers, he never went hunting without his Subaru. I found it kinda strange that the hunting cabin only had a small air strip behind it and no place to drive a Subaru."

Natalie stared at Sarah. Had the nosy detective actually found the remote cabin? Impossible. Yet, the evidence seemed clear. And what about the journal? Her face went pale. "I'm...glad you're...doing your job, Detective Garland," she managed to speak and quickly wiped blood from her lip. "I think I'll go back to my room now and rest. I no longer have an appetite."

"Before you go," Sarah said adding gas to the fire, "I want to let you know that I'm going to get a court order that will allow me to review your father's will."

"How dare you!" Natalie erupted, her curly hair practically shaking with anger. "My father's will is a private matter for the family and it will remain private, no matter what illegal court orders you may attempt!"

"Is that why you went to the mayor of Los Angeles and pressed him to jump down the throats of the police on your behalf?" Sarah asked Natalie calmly.

Natalie stared at Sarah. Her mouth worked angrily, as if biting back words, and her cheeks flared an ugly shade of red. All of her plans were suddenly unraveling at the seams. After a moment, she gritted out, "I'm returning to my room," and turned to march outside.

"Sure, go ahead. Tell Chet's wife we'll see her soon," Sarah said in a calm voice.

Natalie stopped walking. She swung around and stared daggers at Sarah. Sarah could see that panic was warring with rage inside of Natalie. "Milton's so-called wife is in Los Angeles, Detective Garland."

"Maybe, maybe not. No matter, I have some very damaging evidence to present to the judge tomorrow morning. After that, I doubt you'll be leaving our town anytime soon. And if Milton's wife is around someplace, I'm sure we'll smoke her out of the shadows."

"Not so tough now, are you?" Amanda grinned at Natalie.

Sarah nudged Amanda's side subtly. "Of course," she said and lowered her tone, quickly looking around to make sure Anne wasn't in earshot, "we could make a deal."

"A deal?" Natalie asked, swallowing down her panic and rage.

"Sit down," Sarah said. She pushed Amanda down into the booth and scooted in beside her. "Play along," Sarah whispered. "Ms. Hopski, please sit down."

Natalie hesitated. But then she seemed to make a decision. She walked over to the booth and carefully sat down. "I'm listening," she said in a cautious voice.

"Listen," Sarah coaxed, looking at Natalie over her coffee mug, "we can all be friends. It's obvious I have enough evidence to at least make a jury think twice about setting you free." Sarah sipped her coffee. "Ms. Hopski, this is a small town. I'm a retired cop and I know everyone. What I say, goes. So..."

"I think I know what you're implying," Natalie said, ready to get straight to the point. She sat back in the booth a little bit, clearly ready to school two backwoods investigators in the ways of bribery and corruption. This was Natalie's familiar ground and she was very comfortable now, all the tension and fury of the earlier altercation forgotten.

"Oh?" said Sarah. "I want to make sure you understand—"

"We have enough evidence to send you up the river, sister," Amanda said, jumping in with both feet. Sarah discretely nudged her best friend under the table to calm her down a little – Natalie needed to think everything was calm and pre-planned.

"You've seen what our humble police department is like,

Ms. Hopski. It's a real struggle in a small town like this. I'm sure you can understand that sometimes investigations get bogged down, evidence gets lost…" Sarah kept her insinuations vague. She could not, under any circumstances, imply that Natalie could buy her way out of this conviction. Natalie had to come up with that ugly bit of skullduggery on her own.

Amanda picked up her coffee and sipped at it almost daintily. "We don't like threats. But sometimes things can be…smoothed over, if you catch our drift."

"That is," Sarah added, "if it's worth the trouble."

Natalie darted her eyes back and forth between Sarah and Amanda. "I think I can make it worth your while, ladies," she said quietly. She was cool and in control, now that she believed that money was the key to ending her problems in Snow Falls.

Sarah kept her poker face still. The trap had shut behind Natalie now, though she didn't even know it.

"We'll have to settle this…elsewhere," Sarah said, glancing around at the other customers. "Privately."

"When and where?" Natalie demanded in a quiet voice.

"My cabin, midnight," Sarah whispered. "Come alone." Sarah fished a pen out of her rain jacket pocket and scrawled directions to her cabin on a napkin.

Natalie snatched the napkin from Sarah's hands. "I'll be there," she said and coughed, and wiped one last tiny trickle of blood from her mouth. "I want both of you present when I arrive. No games."

"No games," Sarah assured Natalie.

"Yeah, no games, sister," Amanda promised. "But you remember this: if you try anything funny, the evidence we have in our possession goes public."

"Perhaps we can talk about the journal tonight, in private?" Natalie said through gritted teeth.

"If you're willing to make it worth our while tonight,

you'll get half of the journal," Sarah told Natalie and drained her coffee. "If you can prove that you're serious, we can make future arrangements for you to get the other half – the most damaging half."

"The half where your father talks about you pushing your mother down a flight of stairs in a department store in my home town of London," Amanda added.

Natalie licked her lips. It was clear to her that Sarah possessed the journal of William Archie Hopski. The old man was causing more problems for her dead than when he was alive. "I'll be there tonight. No games."

"You better be," Sarah said speaking in a tough voice. "I'll play nice, Ms. Hopski, until you play foul. Let's not take that route, okay? The choice is yours."

"It's either prison," Amanda promised, "or..."

"I know what you want. What choice do I have?" Natalie hissed, without realizing that she was indicting herself in public. "I'll arrive at your cabin at midnight, Detective Garland." Natalie stood up. "All cops are dirty," she said in a disgusted voice. "You're no different than a street cop taking a payoff from a sewer rat."   .

"Hey, a girl has to make a living," Sarah said and motioned at the front door. "Midnight, Ms. Hopski, and not a minute later."

Natalie glanced down at Amanda. "Never touch me again, is that clear?"

"Take a hike," Amanda snapped at Natalie. Natalie was about to snap back, but thought better of it when she spotted Anne walk out of the kitchen carrying two plates of food. Instead, she turned an evil eye at Amanda and hurried out into the storm. "The trap is set," Amanda said in an excited voice. "Sarah, love, you're brilliant."

"You didn't do so bad yourself. And wow, you sure let that woman have it." Sarah grinned at her best friend. "I'm impressed."

Amanda blushed. "I don't know what came over me. I...saw red and the next thing I knew I was on top of her."

Anne approached the booth. "I saw the fight," she said and placed their dinner plates down onto the table. "My husband wanted to come up here and break up the fight, but I wouldn't let him." Anne winked at Amanda. "Not bad, girl. Not bad at all."

Amanda blushed again. "Well, you know...sometimes us quiet little English people can be full of fireworks when the situation calls for it."

"I bet," Anne said, proud of Amanda. She patted Amanda on the shoulder and walked away.

Sarah smiled, picked up a dinner fork, and looked down at her hot plate filled with delicious chicken and dumplings, green beans, okra, and a dinner roll. "I'm starved. Let's eat."

Amanda grabbed her fork and tore into her food. "So, what is your plan, Los Angeles?"

"Natalie thinks she's cornered us, that we're a couple of greedy small-town cops looking for a payoff. She isn't going to show up at my cabin alone," Sarah explained, taking a bite of her food. "I intend to catch all the killers with one net tonight."

"Do you really believe Milton's wife is Natalie's sister?" Amanda asked.

"I do," Sarah nodded her head and picked up her dinner roll. "I also believe Natalie has a brother that's lurking around here somewhere." Sarah took a bite of her dinner roll and looked out at the storm. "Tonight, June Bug, we turn into the hunters."

"For Mr. Hopski's sake, let's hope we snag the game we're after," Amanda said and continued to eat her dinner. Outside, the rain continued to fall.

Andrew didn't like Sarah's plan. No, not at all. But what could he do? He now had two dead bodies in his town and feared the count might rise if immediate action wasn't taken, beginning with Sarah and Amanda. He caved in and listened to Sarah explain her plan. "Keep Milton and Chet behind bars," Sarah warned Andrew before leaving his office. "I'm not sure, but Natalie might try to get to them if she thinks she has some high ground to stand on. I doubt she would actually attack them here at the police station, but she might."

"So, that means you want me to stay here at the station, right?" Andrew asked in a reluctant voice. He looked down at the open take-out container of chicken and dumplings on his desk, snatched up his dinner roll, and morosely took a bite.

"Andrew, I need you to trust me," Sarah explained. "I'm giving Natalie enough time to send someone out to my cabin to watch it before Amanda and I arrive. I want Natalie to think that I'm really about to take a bribe to let her go free and hand over her father's journal," Sarah plopped down in a chair. "We've got a few more minutes. Let's go over the information you dug up on Natalie, okay?" She flipped open a folder full of notes and started asking him questions in between his mouthfuls of dinner.

Meanwhile, Amanda was in the holding cell area, talking to Milton and Chet through the bars. Milton and Chet sat on one of the cell's cots, drinking coffee and eating apple pie from take-out containers she had brought them from the diner. Being arrested, Milton informed Amanda, wasn't so bad. "You're not really under arrest, guys," Amanda reminded him, "you're under protective custody, remember?"

"Well, it sure looks a lot like jail, doll face. When do we get our stripey orange pajamas?" Milton joked, but his brother didn't even smile.

"Hopefully this will all be over soon," Amanda said, trying to give Chet an encouraging smile.

Chet took a bite of apple pie and nodded his head. "Chief

Andrew said he found out that Natalie has a biological brother and a sister. Teresa, my wife, is Natalie's blood sister." His eyes were full of pain.

"I'm sorry, big guy, I truly am," Amanda replied in a caring voice. "I know you're hurting and I wish I could take away your pain. Sarah and I were even considering asking you guys to move to Snow Falls and start a new life, leave all your heartache in Los Angeles behind."

"Nah," Milton said as he forked up another bite of his apple pie, "I'm not a snow person. I get cold when the weather drops under seventy-two degrees. But thanks for the offer."

Chet looked up at Amanda. "I don't like the snow either. I like taking walks on the beach in the warm sunshine."

Amanda nodded. "Don't count yourselves out just yet, boys. You know, I never thought I'd move to Alaska, but the snow is like home to me now. I actually kind of start missing it after a while. Of course, when winter does arrive, all I do is complain, fuss and gripe. But deep down I love every single snowflake that falls out of God's beautiful sky." Amanda smiled. "I wasn't always fond of the snow. My first winter in Snow Falls was a disaster. I ran my truck into a tree, hit trash cans, slipped on sidewalks, you name it, I did it. But eventually I learned how to live with the snow and the snow learned how to live with me."

Milton sighed. "I guess Pop liked the snow, too...and so did Ma. I wish...I wish Pop had invited us to Alaska with him. All these years we thought he was hunting in Africa. He made his trips sound so convincing...he even showed us photos."

"Fake photos," Chet pointed out.

"Yeah, I get that now," Milton nodded his big head slowly. "I wonder why Pop never talked about the cabin?"

"Some things are deep and private," Amanda ventured. "Love can be a wonderful dream as well as a painful tear that people hide within their hearts. Maybe your father didn't want people to see his tears?"

"I wouldn't have minded seeing Pop cry," Milton said quietly and looked down at his apple pie. "I know Pop was emotional at times. After the nightmare he went through in the war, who could blame the guy?"

Chet reached over and patted Milton's shoulder. "Maybe I can come live with you, huh?" he asked. "I don't like living alone. Your condominium is really big."

"Sure," Milton forced a smile to his face, "we'll be two swinging bachelors. We'll order pizza every night and guzzle down Pepto Bismol afterward."

"Okay," Chet smiled back.

"We'll watch old reruns of Bonanza and Gun Smoke. You like those shows."

"I like Hoss," Chet confirmed and nudged his brother with a loving shoulder. "Daddy would like us becoming roommates and watching Bonanza together."

"Yeah, he would," Milton agreed. He looked at Amanda. Amanda had tears in her eyes. "Hey, kiddo, are you okay?"

Amanda wiped at her tears. "I feel so close to you guys. It's going to break my heart to see you leave. I mean, I know Los Angeles is your home, but I wish you would both stay."

Chet looked at Milton. Milton looked at Chet. They didn't know what to say to a crying woman; not a clue in the world. "We could live here during the summer months," Milton suggested.

Chet nodded his head. "The apple pie is really good, and so is the coffee."

"And it won't be like we're leaving Los Angeles altogether. And who knows, maybe we'll even like it up here. Pop and Ma sure did."

"You mean it?" Amanda asked in an excited voice. She wiped at her tears. "You guys will consider living in Snow Falls during the summer months?"

Chet smiled at Milton. Milton gave a thumbs-up to Amanda. "You got it, kiddo. Milton and Chet Hopski will make your little town their home three months out of the year."

Amanda beamed. "I know a cabin that's for sale. The cabin isn't huge, mind you, but it's a comfortable size. We can get you some furniture and a truck and—"

"Slow down," Milton winked at Amanda, "first let's make sure we make it through this night alive."

"Oh...oh, yeah," Amanda said and smiled. "You guys sit tight. You sure have made me happy with this news! Wait till Sarah hears. I'll be back for you when the coast is clear."

"Are you sure you know what you're doing?" Chet asked Amanda worriedly. "Natalie is a very dangerous woman. And together with Teresa..."

"It looks like you have a good old-fashioned family reunion on your hands, kiddo," Milton pointed out.

"Sarah and I are pros at dealing with low-lifes," Amanda promised. "You guys just enjoy your apple pie and coffee and leave the bad guys to us." Amanda waved goodbye and hurried back to Andrew's office. She found Sarah talking to Andrew about Natalie's siblings. The good news about the Hopski brothers turning into Alaska snowbirds would have to wait. "Well, catch me up on the news?" she asked, stepping into the office and sitting down.

"Natalie's biological brother is a man by the name of Brent Dedd," Sarah told Amanda. "Brent Dedd is forty-nine years old, no wife, no children, and no current job. His last known address was in Louisiana, but he left there two years ago and vanished into the wind."

"Sarah believes that might be around the time Natalie Hopski made contact with Mr. Dedd," Andrew pointed out.

Amanda shrugged her shoulders. "Who knows? I would place my bets with Sarah, though." Amanda looked at Sarah. "Okay, partner, what else do you have?"

"Brent Dedd served in the Air Force. He was a pilot but got kicked out for alcoholism. He began working as a crop duster in the southern states for a few years but ended up having his license revoked when he was arrested for flying intoxicated."

"I see," Amanda said, her eyes lighting up. "You found our pilot."

"Mr. Hopski also had a flying license," Sarah pointed out and pointed at Andrew. "Andrew has been burning up the phone for us."

"Just doing my job," Andrew said in a humble voice finishing off his container of food. "Good stuff," he said and patted his belly. "God is good to feed me tonight. I'm sure grateful."

Sarah smiled. "God is good all the time. If only the diner's kitchen was quite so reliable."

"Amen to that," Amanda chuckled. She told Sarah and Andrew about Milton and Chet agreeing to move to Snow Falls during the summer months.

"Well," Sarah said, thinking, "maybe spending time with us will be good for Chet. His wife is probably going to spend the rest of her life behind prison bars. I feel so awful for Chet."

Andrew pulled a slice of apple pie over and pushed his dinner container into the garbage behind his desk. "Yeah, the poor guy will take a hard hit to the gut when that happens," he said as a clap of thunder roared outside. "Maybe the wife and I will have him over for dinner one night."

"That would be nice," Sarah replied. "As far as I can tell, Teresa has a long criminal history that I don't think Chet is aware of. She had a cover story of being pretty squeaky clean by the time they met and got married."

Amanda turned to Sarah. "Correct me if I'm wrong, but it seems that Natalie Hopski wants all of her father's money for herself, and if her sister Teresa and her brother Brent helped her, they're probably all planning to split the Hopski inheritance, right?"

"That's how it appears," Sarah nodded.

"What about their biological parents, Los Angeles? Did we ever find out who they might have been? I mean, obviously they're either really old or maybe even dead by now, but I'm curious as to who they were."

"I haven't gotten that far," Andrew apologized. "My brain has been running on fumes, ladies. I've spoken to more folks today than I care to admit, and some of those folks weren't really happy to hear from me, if you catch my drift. You would not believe the kind of attitudes I heard today."

"I lived in London," Amanda reminded Andrew. "I've met my share of snobby Brits who hold their noses up above the fog."

"Los Angeles isn't exactly a breeding ground for manners either," Sarah pointed out. "When I lived there I suffered from road rage for so many years, I wore out quite a few horns."

Andrew took a bite of apple pie. "Well, here in Snow Falls it's supposed to be nice and quiet. I don't like killers running loose in my town."

"Don't worry," Sarah said, "they're not running loose anymore. I've painted a target on my back and they're coming straight for me." Sarah stood up. "Come on, June Bug, I think enough time has passed. We better get out to my cabin and catch us some bad guys."

"You seem very confident," Andrew stated in a worried voice.

"I am," Sarah tipped Andrew a wink. "I have a secret weapon stashed in the woods."

"A secret weapon?"

"A security vest," Sarah explained and waved goodbye at Andrew, who just gave her a puzzled look in return. "Wait for my call. When I do call, you can come and scoop up the bad guys."

Amanda shrugged her shoulders at Andrew. "Beats me what my friend here is talking about...I wasn't aware she had a secret weapon other than the journal."

"I should have my head examined," Andrew said in a worried voice. "Okay, get out of here and bring me the bad guys. I'll stay here just in case one of them tries to make a hit on our guests."

Sarah took Amanda's hand and walked her out into the hallway. "Okay," she said in a serious voice, "I was a little glib with Andrew because I don't want him freaking out on me and sending the army out to my cabin. The truth is, we're walking into a dangerous situation, June Bug. Natalie intends to kill the both of us."

"I'm not leaving your side," Amanda told Sarah and squeezed her hand. "We're partners, remember?"

"When we arrive at my cabin, matters are going to become very, very dangerous."

"I know," Amanda replied. "I'm used to the danger by now. Remember, I've handled some pretty tough bad guys myself."

"Yes, you have," Sarah smiled and hugged Amanda's neck. "Okay, June Bug, let's get moving. It's a quarter past ten. I want a little time in my cabin before Natalie arrives." Amanda nodded her head and followed Sarah out into the stormy night.

On the way to the cabin, as Amanda navigated her truck out of town and down the rainy, dark street, Sarah explained the plan. Amanda listened carefully and tried to memorize every detail and remind herself that Sarah knew what she was doing. Still, they were both a little worried and the trip, though brief, was tense.

Sarah checked the gun in her ankle holster as Amanda's truck reached the cabin. Sarah's cabin was dark, silent, and saturated with rain. The black hand of night lay heavy on the cabin, and the two women steeled themselves. Sarah looked through the rain-soaked windshield of the truck and studied the night landscape. Somewhere hidden in the darkness were three killers. "Okay, June Bug, easy does it," she said.

Amanda pulled up next to Sarah's Subaru, turned off her truck, and listened to the heavy rain fall. "Here we are," she said in a voice that fought back worry and fear.

"Follow my lead at all times," Sarah reminded Amanda, then crawled out of the truck and ran up to the front door of her cabin. Amanda bravely followed. Moments later, they were inside the cabin, shaking rain off their rain jackets. "Do you think she will really try to kill us?" she asked Sarah.

"No. She wants the journal," Sarah replied, hanging up her sodden rain jacket on the wooden coat rack next to the front door. "She needs the journal, and we've promised half. She wants to kill us, but I think she'll hold off for now because of that other half."

"I guess I'll go make us some coffee while we wait," Amanda said, worriedly. "I just hope you're right and Natalie Hopski plays by the rules tonight."

"I'm confident that she will," Sarah assured Amanda. "When she arrives, it'll only be the three of us. Andrew promised to stay guarding Chet and Milton, so he won't interrupt us. We just have to keep to the plan."

"Okay then," Amanda said, "you're the boss."

"Go make us some coffee and remember to control your temper when Natalie Hopski arrives. We can't afford to antagonize her again. We need what she's bringing us, badly. If she can come through, she might be our ticket out of this dump of a town." Sarah winked silently at Amanda.

"Got you," Natalie said, sitting in a gray van in front of an empty cabin four driveways down the road from Sarah's cabin. She took the headphones from her ears with a satisfied smirk and looked over at the rough-faced man who was also listening in to Amanda and Sarah's conversation through the covert audio transmitter they had planted earlier that evening in Sarah's cabin. "Okay, Brent, once we deal with these two loose ends, we'll be in the clear. Think you can handle them?"

"Just make sure you get them to stand in front of the kitchen window," Brent said and glanced at the high-powered rifle next to him. "Teresa, you stay in the van and pick us up when we call for you."

Teresa nodded in understanding and looked at her siblings with satisfaction. For so long they had been separated, but now they were united by Natalie.

"Okay, then," Natalie said with a dark grin, "are you ready? Because tonight we wrap up this mess, take back what was stolen from us, and walk off into the sunset."

"Finally," Brent snarled. "With the money we're getting, we'll finally get payback. A lot of people are going to suffer."

"Yes," Teresa said, a kind of mad glee animating her features. She shifted in the shadows of the van. "Beginning with Milton."

chapter eight

Natalie walked up to the front door of Sarah's cabin holding an umbrella over her head. Before she knocked on the door, she studied the rainy night with careful eyes. Brent was in place. Teresa was in place. No one else was around in the desolate night under the rain of the spring storm. All that was left to do was tie up a few loose ends. "Your reputation concerned me," she muttered, "but now I know you're just a dumb cop like the rest of them. Money talks to every cop." Natalie raised her powerful right fist and knocked on the front door.

"Follow my lead," Sarah whispered to Amanda, checked the gun in her ankle holster again, and then answered the front door. Rain and wind struck her face. "Right on time," she told Natalie as she stuck her head outside and squinted in the darkness, searching the night. "I assume you came alone?"

"Of course," Natalie snapped. "May I come in?"

Sarah hesitated as her eyes continued to search the rain-soaked darkness. She stood very still for a very long time; long enough to annoy Natalie. Finally, she spoke. "Inside."

Natalie stepped through the front door, closed her

umbrella with annoyance, and saw Amanda holding a gun. "What is this?" she demanded.

"She's alone," Sarah told Amanda. "Go into the kitchen and get us some coffee."

Amanda lowered the gun in her hand, stared at Natalie, and walked off toward the kitchen. Natalie waited until Amanda left before speaking. "I have your money," she said and indicated the hefty black briefcase that she carried. "Now where is my half of the journal?"

"Not so fast," Sarah said, staring at the black briefcase with her eyebrows raised. "We need to talk. Sit down." Sarah pointed at the living room couch. The thought of having a slimy criminal like Natalie in her home made her want to bathe the cabin with bleach. "Take off your rain jacket first, huh? I don't want my couch getting wet."

Natalie reluctantly set the briefcase down on the floor, removed her jacket, and hung it up. "No games," she said quickly and grabbed the briefcase up off the floor.

"No games," Sarah assured Natalie and pointed at the couch.

Natalie nodded her head, walked over to the couch, and sat down. "I want this transaction to take place very quickly, Detective Garland."

Sarah nodded her head, casually bent down as if she was going to scratch her ankle, and yanked out her gun. "First," she commanded Natalie, aiming the gun at her, "show me your recording device. Right now."

Natalie's face went pale. The expression in Sarah's eyes was intense. Natalie slowly reached under the bottom of the briefcase and pulled off a small black recording device no bigger than a dime. "I have to be careful, you understand," Natalie explained in an accusing tone.

Sarah knew that Natalie felt clever. She wanted to make Sarah believe the hidden device attached to the briefcase was all there was. Sarah snatched the recording device from Natalie's hand. "Who is listening on the other end?"

Natalie swallowed. "I—"

"Don't lie to me," Sarah growled. "I'm not a stupid woman, Ms. Hopski. I know you're not working alone. Now, who is on the other end? Your hired killer?"

"I..." Natalie swallowed again. She was prepared. "My employee, yes," she finished, attempting to sound calm and strong.

Sarah lowered her gun a little but kept it trained on Natalie. "I said no games. That is strike one and two. Don't take a third swing, Ms. Hopski. If you do," Sarah shook her head, "you will not leave my cabin alive. Now open the briefcase and let's see what you've brought."

Natalie watched as Sarah slipped the listening device into the front pocket of the dress she was wearing. "Yes, of course," she said and slowly opened the briefcase. "You can count the money if you want."

Sarah stared down at the briefcase. The sight of the neat stacks of hundred-dollar bills made her sick. There had to be hundreds of thousands of dollars in the briefcase. "Amanda will count the money later. Close it."

Natalie closed the briefcase. "Where is my half of the journal?"

"Not so fast," Sarah stated. "First, I want some answers."

"That wasn't part of the deal."

"Then take your money and get out," Sarah pointed to the front door. "I'll go see my friendly neighborhood judge first thing in the morning and let him take a look at the journal and get a court order for me to review your father's will. Then I think I'll find all the motive I need to convince him to issue a warrant for your arrest. For murder."

Natalie's cheeks turned an ugly red. "What answers do you want?" she hissed.

"Why did you kill your father, Ms. Hopski?" Sarah asked. "And why here in Alaska and not in Los Angeles?"

Natalie wrestled with emotions that contorted her face in a hideous way. Sarah could see that she badly wanted to reveal everything, because she believed that she was safe. She believed that Sarah and Amanda would never leave this cabin alive.

She finally spoke. "Los Angeles was too risky," Natalie said. "I was forced to get that old man away from those two stupid monkeys he calls sons."

"Why kill him? He was very old and would have died soon enough," Sarah pointed out.

"Exactly," Natalie hissed. "That stupid old man changed his will on me. I had to act or else. You see," Natalie narrowed her eyes, "William Archie Hopski excluded me from his will. He was a miserly old man. I would have been left with nothing more than the pittance I get from the trust fund each month."

"I understand you receive a large amount of money each month."

"Pennies, mere pennies," Natalie huffed. "I deserve far more. There was no way I was going to let Chet and Milton take my money away from me after our father's death. Drastic measures had to be taken, Detective Garland." Natalie leaned back into the cushions of the couch a little, clearly relaxing into her story.

"I see," Sarah replied, swallowing her disgust. "Tell me, where is Mr. Hopski's green Subaru? I didn't see it anywhere near the cabin."

"I drove the Subaru to a private parking garage. I had to make Chet and Milton believe that backstabbing old man went on another one of his hunting trips."

Sarah paused, thinking over this. "Ms. Hopski, maybe it's the old detective in me, but I am very curious to find out how you discovered Mr. Hopski was, in fact, taking trips to his remote cabin instead of going on hunting trips?"

Natalie watched Sarah with the air of a spider waiting in her web. Natalie believed Sarah was fishing for answers that she would carry to the grave. "William Archie Hopski hated to fly, or so I always believed. But one day I found a repair bill for a private plane he owned. He was a liar, always hiding away from me, always turning everyone against me. Well, this was finally proof. Needless to say, I employed a private investigator to begin following my target."

"I see."

Natalie raised her chin almost proudly. "My...employee...took photos of William Archie Hopski making several visits to the office of his attorney. Now, he may have been old, but he was in terrific health and his mind was still sharp as a tack. I suppose his age would have taken its course soon or later, but once I found out about the visits to his attorney, I knew something was...amiss."

"And drastic measures had to be taken."

"Exactly," Natalie grinned. "So, I had my employee take a few photos of the old man's attorney, photos that were...damaging...and then added a little pressure." Natalie's grin widened. "The man broke and begged me to show mercy."

"Your father's attorney told you of the changes to the will, I assume?"

"Oh yes," Natalie said. "William Archie Hopski had altered his will. And I was no longer in it. Not a penny, not a single cent." Her eyes glazed over with rage at the memory.

"So, you devised a plan?"

"Yes," Natalie stated proudly. "William Archie Hopski had to die, but not before bringing me back into his will, and of course, leaving me as the sole heiress."

"Mr. Hopski's attorney had to be involved."

"That low-life and I made an agreement," Natalie said

with disdain. "I was to have the old man write out a new will and he would make it official."

"And let me guess...your father would end up dead before he could change the will again, right?"

"You're a very bright woman."

"Maybe," Sarah replied. "How did you find out about the cabin?"

Natalie rested her hand on the briefcase. "I got more out of that pathetic attorney than I expected," she said in an arrogant tone. "It's amazing what a few damaging photos can do to a person, isn't it, Detective Garland?"

"Yes," Sarah said and calmly moved forward. "You went through a lot of trouble to make it appear that your father's death was accidental. Why? Why didn't you just kill him and bury his body somewhere near the cabin?"

"Ah," Natalie grinned, "you see, Detective Garland, I had to kill three birds with one stone. Even though I killed that pathetic old man, three thorns remained. Three thorns that could delay me getting my money by challenging the will in a court of law and possibly even causing that weak, miserable attorney of his to change his song."

"I see."

"I had my father state in his will...my new version of the will...that if he was to be found dead, and his death was caused by murder, then his money would go entirely to me." Natalie smiled almost beatifically, and Sarah resisted the urge to slap Natalie across her smug face. "Of course, that's the way I designed the will, but," she admitted, "as I stated, I had three birds to kill. At the moment, some very damaging evidence is hidden in Milton and Chet's condominiums...maps of this area...photos of the cabin...photos of our dear, departed father with red circles drawn around his face...oh, delicious stuff."

"I see," Sarah said, feeling sick to her stomach. "You made it appear that Chet and Milton murdered Charlene and then you were going to frame them for the death of your father as well."

"Yes," Natalie said, poison dripping from her smile. "I wanted the autopsy to prove that William Archie Hopski died accidentally. At least, at first...and then I would lower the boom and finish off my prey."

Sarah sat silent for a few seconds. "What about Milton's wife? Teresa?" she finally asked.

Natalie stiffened some. "She...is taken care of."

Sarah nodded her head. "You do realize that traces of sedatives and hallucinogenic drugs were found in Mr. Hopski's system, don't you?"

Natalie grinned again. "Of course. And poor Milton, the same drugs that were found in our late father's frozen corpse are now hidden under the mattress of his bed. All that is left to do, after our business is conducted, is to make a simple phone call. No loose ends, Detective Garland."

Sarah fought back the urge to bypass slapping Natalie and simply shoot the woman. "Your plan was very well thought out."

"Thank you," Natalie looked into Sarah's eyes. "Natalie Hopski always comes out on top. No one crosses her and lives, Detective Garland. Now, I answered your questions. Let's continue with our business." As Sarah watched, Natalie checked the watch on her wrist with satisfaction. "Perhaps we can have coffee in your kitchen?"

"Sure," Sarah said and stood up and put her gun away. "Amanda can count the money while we have coffee."

Sarah walked Natalie into the kitchen. Outside, hidden in the dark, wet woods, Brent stationed himself behind a tree, aimed his rifle at the kitchen window and waited. "Come on, come on," he said impatiently, "let's get this circus act over with."

Conrad Spencer watched Brent conceal himself behind a tree trunk, wearing a black rain poncho that gleamed in the dark. He silently placed his gun at the ready, and moved forward across the carpet of pine needles on silent feet. "Drop it," Conrad said and pressed his gun up against Brent's back. Brent froze. "I said drop the rifle."

"Okay...take it easy," Brent said, turning into the coward that he truly was. He dropped the rifle. "Hey, don't go crazy on me. This was all my sister's idea, not mine. I'm just—"

"Yeah, yeah, playing along," Conrad said in a disgusted voice. "Put your hands behind your back." Brent did as Conrad said and felt a cold steel cover his wrists. "Turn around."

Brent turned around, fear and cowardice in his bloodshot eyes. He looked into the angry face of a brilliant cop who wasn't in the mood for lies. "I—"

"Who killed William Archie Hopski? Was it you?" Conrad growled.

Brent looked down at the black leather jacket Conrad was wearing. The man was obviously the New York detective who was supposedly absent. "I—"

"The truth," Conrad demanded. He was wet, exhausted and hungry. When Sarah called him after she, Milton and Chet left her cabin the night before and explained the case to him, he had hopped the first flight back to Alaska, arriving back in town just as night was falling. Just in time to help spring the trap. But hey, he thought, feeling relieved he had caught the bad guy, there wasn't anything he wouldn't do for Sarah. After all, the woman was working her way deep into his heart.

"Okay, okay...Natalie and me—"

"And Teresa," Conrad prompted.

"Yeah, and Teresa, we all worked together to get the old man up here into the woods. Natalie slipped a sedative into his drink during dinner and drugged him pretty good. She drove him to the airport where Teresa and me were waiting with my small plane. I flew us out of Los Angeles to Alaska. I made a couple of landings for gas, but no one ever asked questions. It was smooth flying. The field was a little hard to land in, but that was no sweat to me."

"Where is Teresa now?" Conrad asked Brent.

"Parked down the street in a gray van."

Conrad took a small pen flashlight from the pocket of his leather jacket and sent a quick Morse code. Sarah, standing near the kitchen window, saw his signal and smiled in relief. Then she turned her attention back to Natalie who was just sitting down at the kitchen table. "Amanda, count the money."

Amanda slapped down a cup of coffee in front of Natalie with a surly look. But she said not a word, and sat down at the kitchen table, grabbed the briefcase, and began counting the money.

"Where is my half of the journal?" Natalie demanded.

"In time," Sarah said. "Let Amanda count the money. While she is, can you answer me one last question, Ms. Hopski? I would be very grateful."

Natalie glanced at the kitchen window, seeing the clear line of sight from the woods to target the two other women. Soon Sarah and Amanda would be dead. "Yes, what is it?" she asked in an annoyed voice.

"Your so-called employee...or employees, I should say, are people you know personally, right?" Sarah asked. "I did some digging. I know your brother Chet's wife Teresa is actually your blood sister. I also turned up a man named Brent Dedd, another sibling of yours, who, as it turns out, was a pilot in the Air Force."

Natalie tried to control her expression, surprised by Sarah's revelation. "I—"

"You didn't think I would forget about Natalie Hopski, did you?" Sarah asked, remaining calmly at the kitchen window. "Ms. Hopski, I'm always prepared."

Natalie checked the watch on her wrist. Five minutes to

go. "Yes, it's true, Teresa is my blood sister. I arranged for her to marry Chet in order to destroy the man. Milton is no threat to me. He's a weak little man. But Chet is a threat. He's strong and, unfortunately, very smart. I had to keep him occupied."

"Occupied?" Sarah asked.

"Yes," Natalie confessed. "I needed time to locate my biological brother. By the time I located my brother, which was very difficult, I found out about the change to my father's will. You see, my initial plan was to kill Chet and Milton in Los Angeles after I managed to reunite my original family, and then devise a plan to kill off the old man."

"You used Charlene Nelton to manipulate Mr. Hopski."

"That was the easy part," Natalie said snidely. "I promised Charlene power and money and she took the bait. She was supposed to be my 'inside' person, but she failed me. She knew all about the cabin and the change to the will but didn't speak a word, that little schemer. Unfortunately for her, I found out about her plan to double cross me." Natalie's eyes clouded with rage. "So I played her very carefully. I let her think she would be richly rewarded if she helped me make it all happen in Alaska instead of Los Angeles. It was my 'Northern Plan' as Brent began to call it. Charlene jumped on board and handled, well, the useless tasks that I assigned her, such as making Chet and Milton believe their old man had left for another one of his hunting trips."

"You used Charlene Nelton and then killed her when she was no longer useful to you?"

Amanda was still pretending to count the money. She glanced up at Natalie, who watched her contemptuously. "Your stepmother wasn't helpful anymore?" she prompted Natalie helpfully.

"No," Natalie said with a hissing tongue like a snake, "And she was never my stepmother. That skinny little nothing was a power-hungry idiot. Charlene came right up to Alaska as planned, and as soon as I was done with her, I had

Brent drug her with a hallucinogen, make her write that note, and hang her. One bird down, two to go." Natalie looked at the kitchen window and decided to fluff her feathers even more. "And it worked, too. I won. I killed them all, in the end."

"What do you mean?" Sarah asked.

"That journal you found tells the truth. I killed that awful woman who dared call herself my mother. She wasn't my real mother. She never took my side, she called me a liar at every turn and turned my father against me, too. When I pushed her down that flight of stairs, it was with happy hands. Then I killed my father, and now my dear adopted brothers will rot away in prison until they die. I win. I killed them all. Natalie Hopski won the battle. She came out the winner!" Natalie smiled viciously. It was time. She stood up and walked over to the kitchen window. "Detective Garland, may I show you something?"

"Sure," Sarah said innocently. She stood up and walked over to the window. "What is it?"

Natalie grinned. "It's time to die," she said and tapped the kitchen window with the sparkling diamond ring on her right finger, then quickly backed away from the window. Before Sarah could react, Natalie had reached into the right sleeve of her dress and pulled out a tiny, snub-nosed gun. She trained the gun on Amanda, planning to subdue Amanda and march her in front of the window for a second execution. Only, Sarah didn't die. The window didn't shatter with gunfire.

Natalie stared open-mouthed at the window in panic, giving Sarah the opening she needed.

"Not this time, you don't," Sarah yelled. She aimed a hard kick at Natalie's left hand so that the gun spun away from her across the kitchen. As Natalie cursed in pain, Sarah dropped down to one knee, yanked out her own gun, and aimed it at Natalie. "Get your hands in the air. You're under arrest."

Amanda held up a stack of money. "A few hundreds on

top, all fake paper underneath," she told Sarah and tossed the money back into the briefcase. She looked at Natalie and smiled. "But we didn't need your dirty money, anyway. And I guess where you're going, you won't need money, will you?"

"Get her gun, June Bug."

Amanda walked across the kitchen and retrieved the small black gun. "What is this?" Natalie demanded, though the look of panic on her face told Sarah that she clearly knew that her posturing was useless.

A sudden, hard knock on the door answered Natalie's question. "Answer the door, June Bug," Sarah said with satisfaction as she took out a pair of handcuffs and fastened Natalie's wrists tightly behind her back.

Amanda hurried and opened the back door. Conrad appeared, soaked from the rain and plainly tired, but grimly focused on his task. He shoved Brent Dedd and Teresa Hopski into the kitchen ahead of him. Both were handcuffed and hung their heads down, defeated. "Signed, sealed and delivered, Detective Garland," he said and managed a wink followed by a yawn. "Ah, coffee," he said, spotting the coffee pot. "Do you mind?"

"Not at all," Sarah said. And without being able to control her emotions, she then walked over to Conrad and hugged him. Her embrace was fierce and it was a long time before she could let go. Finally, she whispered to him, "Thank you for coming to my rescue."

"Anytime," Conrad whispered back into Sarah's ear, "anytime."

Amanda smiled. Maybe love was in the air. But not for Natalie Hopski, Teresa Hopski, and Brent Dedd. "Alright, you low-lifes, eyes on the floor," she yelled in her best, tough-guy voice. "This romance movie isn't for your eyes."

Sarah and Conrad both laughed as they separated. "I think we have a future cop on our hands," Sarah smiled into Conrad's eyes. Conrad gently reached out to touch Sarah's soft cheek and that one gesture said more to her than words could ever communicate. Then he turned and poured himself a cup of coffee without saying another word. Outside, the rain continued to fall, but the worst of the storm had truly passed. The rain was now clean and healing as it fell on the lush forested hills around Sarah's cabin, and no longer dark and deadly.

Conrad watched Chet dig into a second piece of apple pie. Chet caught Conrad watching him eat and blushed. "I'm making a pig of myself," he said shyly.

"Not at all," Conrad told Chet with a chuckle and pointed to his own empty pie plate. "I've eaten three pieces of apple pie myself." Conrad liked Chet. The guy was okay. He also liked Milton, even though Milton resembled a short mafia boss. Milton, too, was polishing off a slice of apple pie. Conrad grinned at him, "Nice suit."

Milton smiled proudly, puffing his chest out a little in his gray and blue pinstripe suit. "Maybe that doll face detective will notice, huh?"

"Maybe," Conrad grinned. "But let me give you a little advice, okay?"

"Shoot," Milton said and grabbed a glass of cold root beer. "But make it quick, the dames are due to arrive at any moment."

"Dames?" Conrad grinned again. "Uh...never mind, Milton. It seems like you have women figured out better than I do." Conrad leaned back in the diner booth and looked at Chet. Chet shrugged one enormously tall shoulder and continued to work on his apple pie.

Milton took a drink of his root beer. "Ah, what an afternoon. Clear and blue and beautiful as a sapphire. It's going to be a great day for a hike."

"Are you guys sure you want to hike all the way back to your dad's cabin?" Conrad asked. He knew Milton and Chet were both putting on brave faces as city men who had only just recently gotten to know Snow Falls, Alaska. "Sarah told me the cabin is far off the trail. Maybe we should fly you in?"

"We have to hike," Milton told Conrad. "That's why Chet and me are filling our gullets so much. We know our feet are going to cover some miles today, don't we Chet?"

Chet nodded his head. "It's better to be full than to be hungry when you take a hike. Walking burns off calories, too."

Conrad nodded his head. "Yeah, that makes sense. Eat a lot and walk off the food," he said. "I want you guys to be okay, that's all. Today is going to be a very difficult day for the both of you."

"Pop's body is waiting for us in his cabin," Milton reminded Conrad. "It wouldn't be right to fly to his cabin. Chet and me, well…we feel that we owe it to Pop to walk to his cabin, to walk the land he and Ma loved so much."

"Daddy deserves to be respected," Chet said and pushed his pie plate away. "I'll try not to get my suit messy on the walk."

Conrad saw sadness wash through Chet's eyes. "We'll walk slow," he promised and spotted Sarah and Amanda walk into the diner, both wearing warm black dresses and hiking boots. He waved at Sarah. "Are we ready?"

Sarah walked up to the booth. "Andrew is getting our backpacks loaded into the truck now," Sarah explained. "Sorry we're a little late."

"My husband decided to start ringing his bell at the last minute," Amanda explained with a sigh. "It's been back to the bloody bell for me, if it doesn't drive me mad first!"

Milton and Chet smiled. The brothers were starting to feel like a part of the little community and they even liked it when

Amanda fussed about her husband and his bell. "Well," Milton stretched his arms, "there aren't any dames answering to bells where we're walking to, so we might as well get walking."

Sarah looked at Chet. "Guys, I have some news for you before we go."

Chet picked up a glass of water and took a drink. "Is this about Natalie?"

"Yes," Sarah replied.

"Shoot, doll face," Milton told Sarah and winked at her.

Sarah smiled and shook her head. Milton sure was a piece of work. "Natalie Hopski, Teresa Hopski, and Brent Dedd are all going to spend life in prison without any possibility of parole. The evidence we managed to gather is enough to make sure of that."

Chet sighed heavily. "Daddy just wanted us to love each other."

"Yeah," Milton said sadly. "But Natalie was a sour lemon, and I guess a murderer, too. I suppose we should be happy she's going to rot in prison, but I'm glad Pop isn't around to see it. He wouldn't be happy one bit."

Chet looked at Milton. "Maybe Daddy would be happy?" he told his brother. "Daddy believed in forgiveness," he insisted stubbornly. "Maybe his heart was still open toward Natalie. If she was ready to apologize."

"You're probably right," Milton agreed. But he wasn't the type to think about it for long. "Okay," he said and popped to his feet, "no sense in sitting around this diner or I'll just order more pie. Let's move." Milton grabbed Sarah's hand. "You're with me, hot stuff."

Sarah smiled at Conrad. "Looks like I'm taken for the day."

Conrad stood up. "Looks like it," he said and shoved his hands into the pockets of his leather jacket.

"Well, then," Amanda smiled at Chet, "I think I'll take the

company of this handsome man," she said and reached out her hand. "Chet, will you be my hiking partner?"

Chet looked at Amanda's hand and then looked up into her caring, warm eyes. "Okay," he said and stood up to his full, towering height as he gently took Amanda's hand in his own. As he did, he felt a feeling he had never felt before. Not a romantic love – but a kind of safety that comes from true friendship, compassion, honesty and truth. He smiled. "I'm ready to go."

Five hours later, Sarah walked up to the remote cabin with Milton at her side. "Wow," Milton said in pain, wincing as he looked up at the cabin. He stomped over to the front porch steps of the cabin, sat down, and began rubbing his ankles. "That was some walk."

Amanda walked up to the cabin not long after with Chet at her side. Chet was not tired at all. In fact, the hike through the woods and up the river seemed to have given him a renewed air of vitality, causing him to fall in love with Alaska. But when he spotted the simple, polished wood coffin sitting on the far side of the cabin, he stopped smiling. Tears began falling from his eyes. "Is that—"

Chet held up a kind hand to forestall Amanda's reply, and silently walked to the coffin. He dropped down to his knees and bowed his head in prayer, and then his shoulders shook as he cried. Milton stopped rubbing his feet, ran over to Chet, stared at the coffin, and stood very still as tears began flooding from his eyes. "Poor guys," Sarah whispered to Conrad.

Conrad spotted Andrew bringing up the rear with his rifle at the ready and his backpack on. Andrew looked at Chet and Milton, shook his head, and walked over to Amanda and stood quietly. "Being a cop is never easy,"

Conrad whispered and watched Chet and Milton mourn together.

After the burial, Chet and Milton decided to go off on a walk alone to talk about their memories of their father. "We won't go far," Milton promised.

"Maybe you should trail them in case of bears," Conrad told Andrew in a worried voice.

"You got it," Andrew said, and followed the brothers into the woods, keeping a respectful distance.

Amanda hugged her arms. "It's getting late," she commented, watching the shadows on the ground grow darker and darker. "We need to leave soon."

Conrad looked around, searched the woods and saw the beauty of the spring season. He listened to the silence. Then he turned around and studied the old cabin. In his heart, he saw a newly married young couple, desperately in love with each other, standing on the front porch of the cabin, holding each other as the day faded away. He saw the man and woman smiling into each other's eyes while a hot pot of coffee brewed over a cozy fire inside. "A man may have died here, but love was shared here, too," he whispered. For a moment he couldn't speak because of the lump that arose in his throat, threatening to turn into tears.

Sarah looked into Conrad's eyes. "Are you okay?" she asked.

Conrad only nodded his head and turned to let his eyes soak in Sarah's beautiful face. He finally spoke, saying, "I'm grateful you called me."

"I'm grateful you came so quickly," Sarah admitted.

"Did you have any doubt? I only wish you'd called earlier. I mean, Sarah, if I hadn't showed up, Brent Dedd would have shot you and Amanda."

Sarah gently touched Conrad's cheek. "I didn't doubt you for a second," she said and then suddenly realized that her hand was lingering on Conrad's cheek and pulled it away. "A good cop is always on time," she said and looked down at her hands.

Amanda grinned at Conrad. "I think I'll catch up to Andrew. You guys don't lag behind too long."

Conrad watched Amanda hike off into the woods, leaving him standing alone with Sarah. "Amanda wants us to get married," he sighed.

Sarah held her breath, almost afraid to hear him speak those words out loud. "That woman is my best friend," Sarah said instead as she looked at the cabin. She found it hard to look him in the eyes just then. "She may fuss about her husband, but they share a special love." Sarah gathered her courage and looked up into Conrad's eyes. "A love...I miss at times." She waited a moment, searching a face that she had come to know so well. "Being divorced is hard," she finished in a soft voice.

"Being a widower is hard, too," Conrad confessed. He gazed into her eyes for a moment more. "Love is hard, Sarah. Life is hard. People are hard." Conrad shook his head and looked up into a gentle blue sky. "But somehow, we make it through each day by the seat of our pants."

"By God's mercy," Sarah corrected Conrad.

Conrad nodded. "By God's grace and infinite mercy," he agreed and then focused his eyes on Sarah. "I think we'll be okay, you and me. We're tough and we can handle our share of bad guys. And who knows," Conrad softly brushed Sarah's bangs out of her eyes, "maybe in time, two broken hearts might find love again."

Sarah smiled into Conrad's eyes. "Maybe," she agreed. In the dwindling light of day, there was nowhere else she wanted to be than by Conrad's side. "We better start walking. It'll be dark by the time we get back to the trail."

Conrad nodded his head and started walking away from the cabin. As he did, he saw Sarah turn her head and look back. "What is it?" he asked.

Sarah stared at the cabin one last time. "Love never dies," she said in a sweet voice. "Even though there's so much hate in the world, I can see that way out here in the Alaskan wilderness, love never dies."

"Tell that to my husband and his bloody bell," Amanda called out from the woods. Sarah and Conrad looked at each other and shared the genuine laughter of friendship – and maybe something more. They turned and walked into the woods to start the long trek back to the old Snow Bear Trail. As they hiked off through the evergreens, a tender fawn walked over to William Archie Hopski's grave and sniffed the single red rose Amanda had carried and laid there. And then the deer laid down, innocent and pure.

more from wendy

Alaska Cozy Mystery Series

Maple Hills Cozy Series

Sweeetfern Harbor Cozy Series

Sweet Peach Cozy Series

Sweet Shop Cozy Series

Twin Berry Bakery Series

about wendy meadows

Wendy Meadows is a USA Today bestselling author whose stories showcase women sleuths. To date, she has published dozens of books, which include her popular Sweetfern Harbor series, Sweet Peach Bakery series, and Alaska Cozy series, to name a few. She lives in the "Granite State" with her husband, two sons, two mini pigs and a lovable Labradoodle.

Join Wendy's newsletter to stay up-to-date with new releases. As a subscriber, you'll also get BLACKVINE MANOR, the complete series, for FREE!

Join Wendy's Newsletter Here
wendymeadows.com/cozy

Made in the USA
Las Vegas, NV
24 November 2023

81432752R00087